INTO THE DARK

Caroline T. Patti

Month9Books

To Georgia McBride, who wouldn't let me run and hide from my dreams.

"Love of mine someday you will die
But I'll be close behind
I'll follow you into the dark."
~Death Cab For Cutie

INTO THE DARK

Caroline T. Patti

Chapter One

Mercy

A TV, bolted high on the wall, buzzes in the background, the faint sound of the local news reporter's voice robotically reciting the events of the evening. "One dead and another in critical condition ... "

The waiting room is empty of people. Plastic chairs line the walls. Magazines are strewn about. How did I get here?

The news reporter continues to speak. "What appears to be a suicide occurred tonight in the alley behind local watering hole, Wally's Pub. Closed for a private party, owner Kate McCrimons had no comment on tonight's event. Relatives of the victim, high school teacher Matteo Andreas, were not available for comment."

It's all coming back to me now. The party. The alley. Seeing Mr. Andreas with the gun in his mouth. *Oh God.*

"Hey, you're awake." Jay stands before me holding two coffee cups.

"Did you bring me here?" I rub my temples with the palm of my hand. My head is pounding.

"You don't remember?" Jay's eyes narrow and tiny creases indent his furrowed brow. He doesn't look at all like his normal goofy self. His brown eyes are concerned and focused intently on me.

I close my eyes and hold my head in my hands. "I feel sick."

"Kate is on her way," Jay continues. He sits down next to me and sets the cups on the table. "Just a warning, she's pretty freaked out."

Tiny waves of nausea roll in my stomach. My mouth is dry and parched. "I'm gonna throw up."

"Shit." Jay jumps from the chair. I can hear him scrambling around the room. The noise is making me feel worse.

Something bangs into my legs. I open my eyes just a little to see a garbage can. Jay sits back down next to me and holds my hair back as the contents of my stomach empty. My stomach clenches as I grip the sides of the can. I hate throwing up. I hate the convulsions, the acid taste that fills my mouth, and the way a single strand of spittle dangles from my lip like I'm a drooling dog. Luckily, this is happening in front of Jay so it's only moderately mortifying. Having known him all my life, he's seen all sides of me: the good, the bad, and the worse.

"Here." Jay slips a napkin into my hands. He rubs my back lightly. "Should I get a doctor?"

Jay kisses the top of my head and I flinch. My head snaps up too quickly and I stare at him while the room around me sways. "What are you doing?" I have to close my eyes again as another wave of sick crashes over me.

He takes his hands off me. "What?"

"Why'd you kiss me?" I peer at him sideways.

"I'm sorry." He says it like a question, and then he looks at me like I'm nuts. "I was just trying to make you feel better, Ly."

"Okay, but … "

He called me Ly. As in Lyla. My best friend Lyla. "Why are you calling me Ly?" My pounding head cannot take this conversation.

"That's what I always call you." Jay shakes his head. His mop of curls swishes along his forehead. He brushes it out of his eyes by raking his hands through his hair. "How much did you drink tonight?"

I'm not quite sure.

The smell of my own sick is singeing my nostrils so even though it makes the room spin, I raise my head to look at him. A few strands of long, dark hair fall across my face. Hesitantly, I reach up and pull a clump around so I can see it better. My eyes cross as I stare at the nearly black hair. *What the hell?* Frantically, I pick at it, like an addict with a fixation.

"Lyla, what are you doing?" Jay asks.

I drop the pieces of hair and smooth them back. "Nothing."

"You're acting really weird."

I'm acting weird? He's the one who keeps calling me Lyla for God's sake!

"Here you guys are!" Lyla's older sister, Kate, speaks with an exasperated tone. "I've been looking everywhere for you. There's like sixty waiting rooms in this place." She takes one look at the garbage in front of me and exhales, annoyed. Being a bar owner means Kate has plenty of experience with vomit. "You okay?"

Slowly, I nod as I slide the can away from me with my feet.

She sits in a chair just across from us. "I brought you some clothes." She holds out a brown paper bag to me and waits for me take it.

"Don't give me any grief about what I picked. I was in a hurry." Kate's appearance is frazzled. Deep brown curls spill forth from the messy bun of hair piled on top of her head. Her feet jiggle up and down. Kate always fidgets when she's nervous.

In the bag I find Lyla's "Crazy for Cupcakes" tee, a pair of jeans, and some flip-flops. *Why did Kate bring me Lyla's clothes?*

"Do we know anything?" Kate asks.

"No," Jay tells her. "We're still waiting for the doctor."

"Is Eric here yet?" Kate asks about my dad.

"Not yet," Jay answers.

My dad is on his way. Relief sinks in knowing that in a few minutes I'll be able to hug him and he'll make everything okay again.

"You want some coffee?" Jay reaches for the cup and holds it out to Kate. He gestures toward me as he says, "I got it for Ly, but I don't think she wants it."

I do not. I hate coffee.

"Sure." Kate takes the cup and sips slowly. She gives me a reproachful look when she says, "You drink too much coffee as it is."

I start to protest, to tell them both that it's Lyla, not me, who insists on stopping every morning at Peet's, but Kate quickly adds, "Well, go change. This isn't exactly the place for heels and cleavage."

Cleavage? I look down and see what she means. I'm busting out of the seams! This isn't my dress. This is Lyla's dress. I would never wear a dress like this. For one thing, it's pink. And it looks like dip-dyed ace bandages wrapped around my body. I hold the bag close to my chest hoping to conceal my heaving flesh. *Wait.* I don't have heaving flesh. And I don't have raven hair. Something is very, very wrong.

"Okay." As I stand to go, I teeter on Lyla's five-inch stilettos. Jay catches my elbow and steadies me.

"You need some help?" he offers.

"I got it." *I think.* I cannot get away from them fast enough. Not only do I feel like I'm going to vomit again, but I also feel like I'm having a mental breakdown. My hair is a different color. My breasts are like cantaloupes. I'm not wearing my own clothes. I swallow hard to push down the panic and a touch of bile.

Kate eyes me suspiciously. "Do you want me to come with you, just in case? You don't look so good."

"I'll be fine," I say, hoping to reassure both her and myself.

I don't have much confidence that I can walk far in Lyla's shoes. For a split second I think about going barefoot, but decide against it. Luckily, it turns out the bathroom is just across the hall.

Lyla's dress clings to me like Saran Wrap. I must look like Bambi learning to walk as I concentrate on putting one foot in front of the other. The carpet of the waiting room isn't that treacherous, but the slick, overly polished hallway isn't as forgiving. My left ankle rolls and I stumble just as I reached the bathroom door. *Damn!*

The bathroom is dark. I flip the wall switch and the light flickers, groans, and burns nearly out, casting a ghoulish yellow glow of light over the room. "Great."

I grope my way toward the sink. It is then that my eyes adjust to the dark, and for the first time I see my reflection.

Only it isn't my face peering back at me. It's Lyla's, my best friend since the third grade. Leaning in closer, I stare, mouth agape, into the mirror. Her blue eyes are rimmed with multiple coats of black eyeliner. The red of her lipstick is faded, leaving her lips with only a hint of berry stain. My hands explore, skimming the sides of her cheek, hoping, praying that at any second the illusion will shatter. Despite my desperate hopes, the reflection never morphs from Lyla's into mine.

I rack my brain trying to piece together everything that happened tonight. It's my birthday I suddenly remember. We were having a party at Kate's bar. A party I didn't want. Lyla had talked Gage into being my date. Well, more like forced. But we were having a good time. He's really nice. I went outside; I remember that part. And my teacher was there, that letch Mr. Andreas, and he grabbed me. He kept saying all this weird stuff to me and I tried to get away and that's when Gage came out and started yelling at him. Mr. Andreas had a gun. And he … and he …

I remember the sound of the gun going off, and the brief second of relief I felt when I realized he hadn't shot Gage. But then I saw all the blood. There was so much blood.

I stagger backward knocking into the stall door. It swings open and I drop to my knees over the toilet. I heave and heave, but nothing comes up. I curl into a sitting position. My fingers knot into my hair.

When I finally stand up, I expect—okay hope—that everything will have returned to normal, that I'll be me again, and that seeing Lyla was just some sort of weird post-traumatic stress thing. But when I look in the mirror, I don't see me. I see her.

This isn't possible. There's no way. I must be dreaming.

That's the only explanation. This is just a dream. A very strange, twisted dream.

But it isn't a dream. I press my hand to the mirror. It's solid. It's real. This is really happening.

"Shit! Shit! Shit! Shit! Shit!" I curse as the mother of all freak-outs rumbles inside me. *What am I supposed to do now?*

Chapter Two

How did this happen?
I know that at some point I am going to have to leave this bathroom, but I can't bear to face anyone. What will I say? It's not like I can just walk up to everyone and calmly (okay, hysterically) tell them that I'm not Lyla, that I'm Mercy.

Mercy Clare: sixteen, daughter of Eric and Molly, average grades, average height, average bust size. That's me. I look again at Lyla's reflection. Not this. I am not this.

I peel off the dress. Seeing Lyla naked is shocking. Our bodies can't be more different. Lyla is tone and fit. She has muscles and sizable breasts. I am shorter, softer, with features less developed than hers. I fumble with the straps of these stupid heels nearly falling over. My hands are trembling and I can't make them work. Violently, I yank the shoe off and hurl it at the wall. It bounces and skids to a stop.

I stare into the mirror, stunned and stupid. Like being buried alive, I'm trapped in a tiny space with no possible means of escape. I want to claw at her skin, to peel it from the bones.

"Get a grip, Mercy," I speak aloud to Lyla's reflection. "You'll figure this out."

Dressed and ready, I step back out into the hall and head to the waiting room. My dad is there. His clothes are rumpled and his hair sticks up at odd angles.

It's a struggle not to rush to him. I will him to look at me. *Please, Daddy, please look at me. See me! Know something is wrong. Please.* He does look at me, at Lyla, for a split second, but he only smiles thinly before staring at the floor again.

I can't just stand there gawking at him, so I do what Lyla would do: I sit next to Jay. He takes my hand, intertwines his fingers with mine, and lightly kisses my knuckles. Like a bullet I shoot from the chair.

"What's wrong?" Jay looks startled, concerned.

"Huh? Nothing." Other than the fact that he's my best friend's boyfriend and he just kissed my hand!

Tears threaten at the corners of my eyes. I know what I have to do. I have to tell them. There's no way I can handle this by myself, so why not just shout it out? Sure, they'll think I'm crazy at first, but I'll get them to believe me. I'll make them believe me.

Just as I open my mouth, a woman holding a clipboard enters the room.

"Mr. Clare?"

"Yes." My father looks hopefully at her.

"Dr. Mason would like to speak with you. Would you mind following me?"

He nods. And nods. And nods. But he doesn't move right away. The air in the room evaporates and my lungs squeeze together as I watch him slowly stand. He doesn't say anything to us. He looks so much older than he did just a few seconds ago. He's stooped and shuffling behind the lady as they disappear out of sight.

No one speaks while we wait. I pace around the room while the clock on the wall ticks for an eternity. And then it ticks some more.

I hear shuffling in the hall, and I know it's my father coming back into the room. I clamp my hand over my mouth when I see him. His eyes are rimmed with red. He swallows and starts to speak, but we know. We all know.

"They lost her." He sobs.

My knees buckle.

Kate and Jay huddle around me. We join in a collective state of stupor as the reality of Dr. Mason's message takes hold.

Jay and Kate both cry. Two of the most stoic people I know are crumbling. Kate squeezes what little air I have left right out of me. Jay mumbles, "Oh, my God," over and over.

I want to tell them the truth. I want to make their pain go away. But what can I say? We are mourning the wrong person. I'm not dead. Lyla is.

Or is she? Oh, my God, Lyla! I hadn't even stopped to think about her. Panic sweeps over me as a million questions, none of which I can answer, torture my thoughts. *Lyla, where are you?*

Did I do this to her? On top of everything else, I now feel sinking, strangling guilt.

My attention snaps back to the moment as Dr. Mason asks my father if he has family he can call. I realize there's no one. It's been just the two of us since my mom died six years ago.

I want to scream, "His family is right here!" But what good

will that do?

My feet glue themselves to the floor. Eventually, my whole body, Lyla's body, goes numb.

Over the next few minutes several different hospital staffers, including a chaplain, stop by to speak with my dad. All offer their condolences before handing him flyers about grief and asking him to sign documents. The last lady that comes by, a plump, squishy woman with a rat's nest for hair, wants to discuss arrangements for *the body*.

My body.

"There's several options available to you." She speaks softly, but it feels like she is screaming in my ears. It's wrong, so utterly wrong that she is calmly, casually giving my dad a sales pitch. "We have a lovely selection of caskets and there's always the option of cremation."

Cremation? Did she just say cremation? Will my father even consider that? The picture of myself burning and melting in a blazing fire is enough to jolt me back to life. I bolt toward the exit.

"Lyla!" Jay calls out to me, but I am too far gone to stop.

Chapter Three

I run from the waiting room, down the hall, and into the stairwell like an Olympic sprinter, not stopping or even slowing until I reach the far corner of the parking lot. Lyla's lungs fill with air as her muscles pump and tense in a way that mine never do. She is agile and the sensation of running gives life to her body. She moves gracefully, steadily, whereas I lumber when I run, held back by my short stature and tiny frame.

The endorphins wear off and I collapse into a heap of exhaustion as the breakdown I've been suppressing floods forth. Black trails from Lyla's mascara-drenched tears stain her cheeks.

Everything about wearing someone else's skin gives me the shivers. It's wrong, like an ill-fitting costume. These are her arms and legs, her hands, even her tears. I don't want to be in her body anymore. But I don't want to be dead either. I'm not ready to let go of my life, my friends. *I'm only sixteen!* Too young to die. We are both too young to die.

"Lyla!" I hear Jay's voice calling in the distance. "Ly!"

The thing is, Jay isn't just Lyla's boyfriend. He's my next-door neighbor and one of the best friends I've ever had. He's the perfect combination of sexy and dorky. Nerd chic, Lyla calls it. Jay's the guy who trips over a bump on the sidewalk, spills drinks down the front of his shirt, but doesn't get embarrassed by it. And when he smiles at you, it's like no other person in the world exists. When he finds out that I'm not Lyla it's going to crush him.

What if he hates me forever?

Maybe I don't have to tell him. Maybe I can go on being her forever. It wouldn't be so terrible. Lyla is smart, a good athlete, everyone likes her. We've borrowed everything from each other over the years. Is this really that different?

If I pretend to be her, I get to keep Jay and Kate and even my father, in a way. The loss won't be too great. Of course, I'll lose Lyla. That in itself, might be too much.

Jay slows his steps, approaching cautiously. With his right hand tucked into the pocket of his jeans, his head bent slightly, he looks at me with his dark chocolate eyes. There is so much love, so much intensity in his expression. It is in complete contrast to his unruly curls that fall this way and that, carefree and loose. Looking at him I know that I can't pretend to be Lyla. I can't do that to him. I can't do that to her.

I have to tell him the truth.

Rising to my feet, I dust myself off. Jay bridges the gap between us, takes my hands in his and holds them to his chest as he leans his forehead into mine. My throat constricts as my pulse quickens. Can he feel the hesitation coursing through me?

"I'm really sorry, Ly." His voice catches. "I get it," he continues. "This is a lot to deal with and I'm here for you. Whatever you need."

You can trust him. Just tell him. Repeating this chant to myself, I try to work up the nerve. But what if he doesn't believe me? What will I do then? Standing this close to him, heat radiating from his chest, the comfort of it makes me falter, gives me time to reconsider. Is it so wrong to want this feeling of safety to last a bit longer?

There's a moment before two people kiss when the world stops. Breathing is put on hold, eyes close and lips part in anticipation. Truthfully, I like it better than the actual kissing, that brief second before the lips meet.

That delicious moment is happening to me.

Jay's eyes close as he tilts his head. My body, Lyla's body, reacts before my brain can stop it. The first brush of his lips is timid, patient. But before I know it our lips tangle in a delightful dance of push and pull.

Suddenly, abruptly, I shove him back, and without thinking I hear myself blurt out, "I'm not Lyla! I'm Mercy!"

Jay steps back, shaking his head in disbelief. Before he can speak, I keep going.

"I know this sounds crazy and I know you'll think I'm insane, but it's true. I'm Mercy. I don't know how it happened or why it happened, but you have to believe me! When I woke up, you kept calling me Lyla and you tried to give me coffee, I thought there was something wrong with *you*. But then I went to the bathroom to change and I saw *me*, her. I'm in her, Jay, I'm in her body, but I'm me. I'm Mercy." By the end, the hysteria in my voice is unmistakable. "Please, *please* believe me."

"What are you talking about?"

"I'm sorry. I'm so sorry." The tears start and I don't bother to wipe them off.

"I don't know why you're saying this, Ly, but you need to stop. Just stop."

"I can't. I wish I could, but I can't. When I woke up I was her. And I wanted to tell you, but then everything just happened. Kate was there and then my dad and then that stupid doctor came in and told everyone I'm dead. And I lost it. I mean you're not supposed to be around to watch what happens when your family finds out you're dead. But I did. And it fucking sucks. But I'm not dead, Jay. I'm still here. I'm right here. I'm Mercy."

"We should go back inside, maybe talk to the doctors." He tries to usher me toward the hospital, but I shove him off.

"NO! There has to be something I can say to convince you. Ask me anything. Anything about me, Mercy, and I'll tell you."

For a brief second his expression changes and I think maybe, just maybe he's beginning to believe. But then he yells, "Stop!" and turns from me.

I go around to face him. Grabbing him by the arms I plead with him. "You know what I'm talking about. You *know*. But I'll say it if that's what it takes."

He breaks free of my grasp and strides a few paces away. He's cracking. I'm getting to him.

"It was the night your parents told you they were getting divorced." Jay's shoulders tense as I speak. "You climbed through my window with a half empty bottle of tequila. We talked all night. I held you while you cried. You were so upset and I was trying to make you feel better. Neither one of us meant for it to happen."

"Stop," he whispers. "Don't say anymore." He doesn't turn around, but I can tell he's processing what I've said.

"You were so drunk that I wasn't even sure you'd remember kissing me. But when you woke up the next morning you started freaking out and you begged me. You begged me not to say anything to Lyla. And I didn't, Jay. I swear I didn't."

Slowly, Jay spins on his heels. When he faces me again his eyes are wide. He studies me, like he's seeing me for the first time. Not Lyla, me.

"Mercy?"

Chapter Four

Gage

Once I reach the parking lot, Lyla and Jay come into view. I think for a second that maybe I'm wrong, maybe it didn't happen. When Jay leans forward and kisses her, hope floods through me. But when she shoves him away I know.

She isn't Lyla. She's Mercy. The worst has happened.

My fingers latch onto fistfuls of hair and I kick a rock, sending it soaring into the hubcap of a car.

"Son of a bitch!"

A surge of guilt and regret rocks my insides. The one thing I've been trying to prevent, Mercy breaching a body, is the one thing I've failed to keep from happening. Things are such a mess now. Facing the others, telling them of my colossal screw up, is only one of the many problems I face. Rae will say I told you so. Maybe not out loud, but she'll think it and she'll give me that look, the one that says, *you should have listened to me*.

Zee will be furious, but of all of them, he'll have the most empathy for me. Jinx, of course, will side with Rae. Jinx follows everything to the letter of the law, he only sees in black and white, no shades of gray.

Rae will mostly be pissed. I let a Breacher cloud my judgment. But she doesn't understand. None of them do. Mercy isn't like any of the other cases we've dealt with.

"You've fucked this up royally." Rae's icy voice makes all the hairs on the back of my neck stand up. "We have to end this now, Gage, before it goes any farther."

Slowly, I turn to face her. Clad in black skinny jeans, motorcycle boots, and a leather jacket that looks as though it was beaten, she stands with her arms folded across her chest. Her right foot is popped out like a dancer's, her standard stance whenever she's feeling superior.

"What do you propose, Rae? That I waltz over there and slit her throat?"

"If you'd rather I do the wet work, that's fine with me."

I let out a quick puff of air before saying, "Just go home. You're making this worse."

Her amber eyes narrow as she scowls. "I'm making this worse?" She scoffs. "That's laughable. You had one job to do, Gage, and you failed."

"You make it sound like this is so easy."

"It is easy. Find Breachers. Kill them. Simple. It's what we do. It's who we are."

"Stop with the guilt," I groan.

"We are Hunters, Gage. We have a duty to protect people. Why can't you understand that?"

"It's not that simple and you know it, Rae."

She steps toward me. "Why this girl? What makes her any better than the rest?"

Unable to hold her gaze, my eyes drift beyond her to where Jay and Mercy are standing. Jay looks frozen, almost paralyzed. Mercy must be trying to tell him what happened.

Shit. This is getting out of control. I need to get rid of Rae and find a way to talk to Mercy without being seen.

Rae puts her hand on my shoulder. "You're not going to answer my question are you?"

"What question?"

"Jesus Christ, Gage. You need to pull your head out of your ass and focus. Nathaniel is still out there somewhere. He's already murdered one human tonight. What if he's taken another body? Did you think of that, or is your precious Mercy all you think about anymore?"

"I don't have time for your judgment, Rae. She doesn't know what's happening to her. She didn't ask for this!"

Mercy and Jay retreat to the hospital just as a police cruiser pulls into the parking lot.

"I have to go, Rae. You can yell at me all you want later, but right now, I have to help her."

"She's a Breacher. Not some charity case. You need to do your job. Kill her, and all of our problems with Nathaniel are over."

"Rae, listen to yourself. Do you hear what you're saying? You act as if murdering an innocent person is … "

She cuts me off. "Not innocent, Gage. She's a soul-sucking, body-snatching Breacher. Do you know what will happen to you if The Assembled finds out about this? For all we know they're on their way here now."

I wave her off. "I'm not worried about them."

"They'll take your powers, Gage. They'll turn you into a human. You'll be mortal. Is that what you want? To die?"

She takes a breath and softens her stance. "You'll end up like Nathaniel."

Everything she says is like a new bullet to an already hole-ridden target. I'm hanging on by a thread and I know it. Facing The Assembled won't be easy. If they turn me human, cast me out, I don't know what I'll do or what I'll become. But as much as that terrifies me, I can't turn my back on Mercy.

"Rae, I'm sorry. I truly am. I know I can't make you see, can't make you understand why I need to do this, so I'm asking you to trust me."

"I have trusted you. And that led us here. You think she's different, or that you can change her, but you're wrong. Look what she did! The first chance she got she took her best friend's body. Are you even considering that?"

"It was an accident and you know it." I meet her glare with full force. "Rae, you know it. Nathaniel grabbed her in the alley and he forced her out of her body. She never meant for this to happen."

"This is all on you now," she spits. "I'm out. If you want to go down, you're not taking us with you. You're on your own."

Though I want this to be one of Rae's many empty threats, her set jaw tells me that she's dead serious.

"Rae, I know I'm asking a lot and I know that I've already made you risk so much, but please, just give me some more time. Let me try and help her."

"No matter what happens," Rae starts, "I'll never understand why her. After everything we've seen and everything we know…" she trails off. Composing herself, she clears her throat and says flatly, "This isn't going to end the way you want. She's a Breacher, Gage. By sheer design she follows only her emotions, her desires. It will overtake her, just as it did for all the others. She'll disappoint you."

"She won't."

Rae rolls her eyes. "Oh, Jesus! You didn't! You're in love with her? Really?" She puts her fingers to her temples. "You're going to get us all killed. The Assembled will come, and they won't just take it out on you, Gage. There will be consequences for all of us."

"I can't talk about this now. I can't say ... I don't know ..." I huff out an exasperated breath. "Please help me, Rae. Find Nathaniel before he does any more damage. Give me a chance to help Mercy."

Rae kicks at the ground, scuffing the toe of her boot. "Fine," she says through clenched teeth.

I grab Rae by the forearms, lean forward and kiss her cheek. "Thank you." Leaving her, I tear through the parking lot toward the hospital.

Chapter Five

Rae is right. I am breaking all the rules. Falling for a human is beyond forbidden. But I'm not even sure that's what happened. I don't know what love is exactly, or what it feels like. All I know is that I have to help Mercy. I have to try. And again, Rae is right. Because of the mess I've made, things are out of control.

Mercy's case was assigned to me six years ago, after her mother died. The Assembled thought maybe the trauma of it would trigger a breach. When it didn't, I went into a holding pattern, watching her from afar. Everything was going according to procedure. I kept my distance. But as I watched her something inside me shifted. I wanted to watch her. I wanted to be near her. It was more than obligation, but I had it under control. Everything was fine. Until Nathaniel showed up.

Nathaniel Black is one of the oldest and most notorious Breachers ever. He's always one step away from our grasp. He infiltrated Mercy's life a year ago, taking the body of one of her teachers, Mr. Andreas. But he didn't act, he didn't confront her, tell her who she was or what she could do. He sat back and watched. And I needed to know why.

It's become an obsession for me, watching him watch her. Recently, I could feel his impatience growing and I knew he was going to strike. *That's* why I stepped in. It wasn't because of how I felt about Mercy. I thought maybe if I could get to her first, learn more about her, then maybe I could figure out Nathaniel's plan.

It was in the school library, just after lunch when my opportunity presented itself. The bell rang and Mercy rose from her chair to repack her bag. A stack of note cards slid through her fingers and fell to the floor.

"Let me help you," I said to her.

"Thanks." She looked up at me, wide brown eyes circled by a ring of dark green.

I extended my hand and introduced myself, "Gage." The corner of her lips pulled into a playful smile and instantly I knew the handshake was a stupid idea.

She shook my hand anyway and said, "Mercy."

"Pleasure." Holding onto her hand too long, I quickly dropped it and tried to act normal.

"You're new? I don't think I've seen you before." She tucked the note cards into her backpack.

"Yes. Just started here, you?" Another stupid move. *Christ, Gage. Stop being such an idiot.*

She laughed, smiled again and said, "Not quite."

The bell rang.

"Thanks again for the help," she said.

As she started to turn, she paused. Her eyes closed, her face contorted, and she swallowed hard. As she swayed, I rushed forward and braced her. She leaned into me and I supported her as her hair fell across her face.

Guiding her toward the table, I slid a chair back with my foot and eased her into it. Like a rag doll, she slumped forward a bit.

Kneeling in front of her I brushed the hair from her eyes and asked, "Are you all right?"

Sluggishly, she nodded. From my backpack I withdrew a water bottle and handed it to her. "Here, drink this."

Her lips parted just enough to swallow a tiny sip. When she finished she said, "I feel dizzy."

"It'll pass," I assured her.

The second bell rang. She looked up at the clock on the wall and frowned. She whispered, her words slurring slightly, "I'm late for class. You're late too. Sorry."

"It's fine." I pulled another chair over and sat across from her. "Do you want me to take you to the nurse?"

She shook her head. "I have a test. I have to go to class."

"What class?"

"Mr. Andreas. World Lit." Her words were slow and drawn out.

Nathaniel. He couldn't see her like this. Mercy's hold on her body was weakening as the Breacher part of her clawed its way to the surface. I didn't know how much longer she had left. Days? Hours?

"Maybe you should skip that one today."

"Mercy!" A tall, strikingly beautiful girl with dark hair and blue eyes called from across the room. The librarian at the desk shushed her. The girl responded by rolling her eyes.

"Lyla." Mercy's speech was still breathy, as if her brain was having trouble processing thought.

"What's wrong? You look terrible," Lyla said.

"Dizzy." Mercy's head popped up for a second then quickly flopped forward.

"Are you drunk?" Lyla asked sarcastically. "'Cause that would be funny."

"She fainted. Sort of. I mean, I caught her before she fully went out," I told Lyla.

She eyed me. "And you are?"

"Gage."

"Well, thanks for helping. I can take it from here." She reached around Mercy's waist and pulled her to her feet. "Come on, birthday girl, up we go." She propped Mercy against herself and pulled her to her feet.

For a second, I thought Lyla had her, but Mercy's legs buckled. I jumped to my feet and threw Mercy's arm over my shoulder. Together, Lyla and I held her up.

"The nurse's office is just down the hall." Lyla nodded to the left. "You better recover by tonight, Mercy. Or I'm seriously going to be pissed."

Surprised by Lyla's statement I said, "You're being a little harsh, don't you think?"

"Maybe." She laughed, which caught me off guard. Continuing, she said, "But she promised me she was going to enjoy this birthday and I'm holding her to it."

"I don't think she's in any condition to celebrate. She can barely stand."

"I'm sure it's just low blood sugar or something, right, Mercy?"

Mercy's head lolled to the side and rested against my shoulder.

"Has this happened before?" I asked, my voice more urgent than I would've liked.

Lyla readjusted Mercy's weight and said with exasperation, "She gets like this around her birthday. She goes all *Girl Interrupted* on me, which I think is just an excuse to sit around and wallow. But not this year. She's going to have fun even if it kills her."

We reached the nurse's office. I forced the door open with my shoulder. Lyla followed, sideways, as we carried Mercy over the threshold. It was just a few more feet to the cot where we carefully laid Mercy on her back.

"Well, what do we have here?" the nurse asked.

I was about to explain how she fainted, but Lyla spoke first. "Low blood sugar."

"You know where the crackers are, Lyla. I'll get her some juice." The nurse disappeared around the corner while Lyla walked over to a cabinet and pulled out a box of Saltines.

"Can you prop her up?" Lyla asked me.

I slid my hands under Mercy's neck and shoulders and leaned her into a sitting position.

"Okay, open up." Lyla took a cracker and held it to Mercy's lips. Reluctantly, Mercy bit down and chewed a tiny piece. "That's a good girl. Now, here comes the choo-choo," Lyla cooed as she force-fed Mercy another piece.

Mercy flashed her a look of annoyance. That was a good sign.

"Here's the juice." The nurse came forward with a carton of orange juice, a straw protruding from the top. "Little sips, remember?"

Mercy drank the juice and the color slowly came back to her face. Her cheeks flushed with a pinkish glow while her eyes brightened back to life. She was definitely starting to look better.

Lyla fed her another cracker. This time Mercy took a

healthy bite and chewed eagerly.

"Thank you," Mercy said.

I exhaled, not realizing that I'd been holding my breath nearly this entire time.

"Feeling better?" the nurse asked. "Or do I need to call your father?"

Mercy shook her head. "I'm okay. You don't have to call." Sheepishly she looked up at the nurse. "Sorry."

"No need to be sorry, hon. But if you start to feel sick again, you come straight back here, got it?" Mercy nodded and the nurse went over to her desk and took out a pad of paper. "I'll write you kids a pass for your next class."

"Thanks, Ms. Dwyer," Lyla responded.

Mercy continued to eat and drink as my anxiety level receded.

"Did I faint?" She quietly asked.

"Yes, but ... " Lyla turned to me, "What's your name again?"

"Gage."

"Right. Gage caught you. You already look better and I'm sure that by tonight you'll be ready to party."

"Ha ha," Mercy said mockingly.

"It's useless to try and avoid it. You're going out and that's all there is to it."

"I don't know ... " I started to protest.

"Gage is worried about you, Mercy. He's quite the knight in shining armor, which leaves me with only one choice. He's just going to have to be your date for tonight."

Mercy and I exchanged a look of utter embarrassment. Her mouth was still full of food, but her expression said it all.

"Um, that's really nice, but I don't think ... " I stammered.

Lyla cut me off. "You don't know me, seeing as we just met. But you should know that I pretty much always get what I want. So there's no real point in fighting this." Lyla shrugged as if the conversation was over.

Mercy swallowed the rest of the cracker. "Lyla!" she said scoldingly. Then she turned to me. "You don't have to, I mean, she's just being, well, her."

"Oh, well, if you don't want me to then … "

"She does, trust me." Lyla smiled mischievously.

"Stop talking about me like I'm not here," Mercy said forcefully. Her strength was returning more quickly.

"So, Gage. How 'bout it?"

"I'd love to."

Chapter Six

Lyla and I walked Mercy back to class, though I made my exit before we actually reached the door. It was not the time to be seen by Mr. Andreas. For the time being it was much better to keep to the shadows.

Keeping an eye on Mercy, learning as much as I could about her, was all part of my plan. The strange sensation that I got in my stomach when I agreed to be her date was not part of the plan. I wasn't supposed to feel *that* way about her.

I knew full well that the other Hunters—Rae, Jinx, Zee—would warn me against going. They would tell me that I was getting in too deep. And though they were right, if I hadn't gone, I might not have been able to save her from Nathaniel.

Accompanying Mercy to her birthday party was a mixture of awkward and awesome. She looked hot in her gray party dress. Her hair cascaded in curls down her back. She smiled at me, trying to keep up the conversation. She was nice to me, and completely unaware of who I was. Under normal circumstances, I would've ended her life without giving it a second thought. But she looked at me and talked to me like I was human. I wanted to touch her, to hold her. I kept imagining the taste of her lips.

The party was in full swing, people dancing and talking and music pumping. I lost sight of Mercy immediately. After fruitlessly searching the room for her, I decided to check the alley. It was there that I saw her, pinned to the wall by Nathaniel—Mr.Andreas.

"Let her go!" I ordered.

Slowly, methodically, he turned toward me, all the while gripping Mercy by the arms. "I should've known you'd come sniffing around."

Mercy and I locked eyes. Fear, confusion, panic, every distressed emotion possible seemed to radiate from her.

"I said, let her go." Cautiously, I crept closer.

Nathaniel released his grip suddenly and Mercy fell to the ground. She flattened herself as best she could against the wall, scrambling to regain her footing.

From his breast pocket, Nathaniel removed a small caliber pistol. The deliberate click of the gun as he pointed it in my direction stopped me in my tracks. Though I've dodged bullets before, my focus was split between myself and Mercy and I didn't trust that I could react in time.

Mercy, still cowering, covered her ears and squeezed her eyes shut.

Nathaniel titled his head to the right, smirking. He knew he had me. He smelled my fear. My heart pounded in my ears, drowning out all other noise. I positioned myself, ready to jump at any moment.

He let out a small, maniacal laugh, shoved the gun into his

mouth, and pulled the trigger.

Startled, I stumbled back and hit the wall. Seconds later, Mercy's whole body began to shake. "Mercy!"

Rushing toward her, I drew her into me. "You're okay. You're okay." I kept telling her.

"He shot himself. He's dead. He's dead," she babbled.

I tried to hold her, but the shaking increased until she broke free of my arms and fell, her knees and hands smacking against the concrete. Acting quickly, I scooped her into my arms and held her tightly against my chest.

"Mercy! Mercy! Look at me!"

Her body convulsed and seized. Her eyes rolled into the back of her head. There were others in the alley now. I could sense them even with my back turned.

"Call an ambulance!" I yelled. "Come on, Mercy. Don't do this. Stay with me. Please."

I'd failed her. I'd failed The Hunters. Violent anger rushed through me. I wanted to pummel Nathaniel, throttle him, tear him limb from limb. He was purposefully messing with me. It wasn't that I didn't expect that kind of thing from him, it was that I was clueless as to why. He could've shot me, wounded me long enough to take Mercy and escape, but he didn't.

Lyla and her boyfriend Jay rushed to Mercy. Though it was agony to leave, police cars and an ambulance roared through the alley and I couldn't stay. In the confusion, I backed away and out of sight, cursing myself and my stupidity the entire time.

***

Fleeing the scene, leaving Mercy there—I hated it. I wanted to be in the ambulance with her. I didn't want to leave her side because I knew what was going to happen. And now, seeing Mercy, or rather Mercy as Lyla, from across the parking lot, confirmed my worst fears. Mercy has breached. It's time to formulate a new plan.

With Rae gone, I slip through the hospital doors in search of Mercy's room, which I find on the fourth floor, ICU. She's unconscious, supported by machines, with, from what I can tell, zero brain activity. Of course the doctors would have informed her family by now that she's dead. For all intents and purposes she is dead, at least to the human eye. Hunters know better.

Her reddish brown hair is matted and caked across the pillow. Her eyes are taped shut. Tubes stick out of her from various portals: arms, chest, stomach. The faint blip from the machine in the corner tells me that Mercy is on life support, her heart kept beating by the machine.

I only have minutes to act. This will go down in Hunter history as the most insane move ever, but I try not to think about that. My thoughts are on Mercy.

Ducking out into the hall I ride the elevators down to the basement to the doctor's lockers. After busting one open, I grab ID and a lab coat and scrubs and rush back to the ICU.

Pulling this off is no easy feat. It's not every day that I steal a body from a hospital.

I unhook her from the heart monitor and quickly duck back out of the room. The alarm sounds and nurses come running. They push fluids into her IVs, pump her chest, shock her twice, but Mercy's body does not respond. They call her time of death at one forty-three AM.

"I don't understand," one of the nurses says. "Did the machines malfunction?"

"It happens, hon," the older nurse replies. "Just add her to the angels."

"So much for organ donation," the first nurse laments. "Such a shame."

Waiting out the next ten minutes is excruciating, but I know I have to keep my cool. When the time is right, I make my move.

"Someone called the morgue?" I say to the nurse at the desk.

"Bed 304," she responds, barely looking up at me.

"Got it. Thanks." I tap the desk and turn to leave.

"Wait," she calls after me. I freeze, my pulse races. "Make sure you take the service elevator. Her family is still in the waiting room."

"Of course."

Once I'm in the elevator with Mercy's body, I flip open my phone and send the text message that I know will spark fury.

    Gage: Rae/meet me at hospital/have
Mercy/hurry.

Rae's car is waiting outside the food delivery entrance. Hoisting Mercy's body from the bed and into my arms, I rush to meet her.

"Now you've just lost your mind!" She slams the door once we're all inside. Mercy lies across the backseat. Rae drives while I ride shotgun.

"I had to. I couldn't just leave her there."

"Yes, you could have." She slams on the gas, tearing through the empty streets at breakneck speed.

"I have a plan. You just need to trust me."

"I'm here, aren't I? I'd call that trust. But that doesn't mean I don't think you're insane."

"Just drive, Rae, I need a minute to think."

Looking into the backseat at Mercy's lifeless body, I question the validity and sanity of my actions. I stole her body. *Jesus Christ!* I'm in over my head.

Chapter Seven

Mercy

Rushing at Jay, I throw my arms around him, nearly knocking him over.

"Whoa," he says. He stumbles backward, trying to support both of us.

"You believe me! I really thought you wouldn't, but you do." I squeeze and squeeze, hugging him with everything I have.

Jay releases me and steps back. "I don't know what to believe. I mean, is this even possible? How? How does something like this happen?"

"I wish I knew."

"Where's Lyla?" His eyes widen. "Is she dead?"

"I don't know," I answer honestly.

"Oh, my God! Is she inside someone else's body?" His hands cling to the side of his head as if he's trying to keep his brain from exploding. "Jesus fucking Christ! How could you just let this happen?"

Stung by his words, my defensive mode kicks into high gear. "You think I wanted this to happen? Like this was some choice I made? What kind of person do you think I am? I wouldn't do that to her, or to you."

His hands slide from the side of his head to his mouth and finally come to a rest at his side. The look of horror, of sadness, on his face is gut wrenching. Knowing that I caused him despair and grief is torture.

"I'm sorry," I tell him. Saying the words does nothing to lessen the agony for either of us.

He shakes his head back and forth, turns away from me, and sinks to the ground. Cautiously, I lay a hand on his shoulder.

Suddenly, Jay pops up. "I thought this day couldn't possibly get any worse. Losing you, when they said you were dead, do you know what that did to me?"

My mouth hangs open. Words escape me. I'd seen him cry for me, but to hear him say how much it hurt leaves me speechless.

"How am I supposed to react to this, Ly ... " He breaks off. "... Mercy. You're not Lyla, you're Mercy."

I nod and hang my head in shame.

"This is too much, you know. I can't ... I don't ... " Jay's eyes fill with tears.

"I'm sorry," I say again.

All the unspoken words hang in the air between us. Though I want to say more, to try to make him feel better, what's the point? He deserves to be angry with me. He's definitely earned the right to grieve, so I think it's best to leave him to it.

I don't know how long we stand there, facing each other, staring at the ground. As uncomfortable as all the not talking is, I know I can't be the one to start the conversation. Being patient isn't exactly a strong suit of mine and the waiting is difficult.

After a while, Jay simply says, "We should get back."

Jay and I walk back to the building and ride the elevator to three. My dad and Kate are still in the waiting room.

"You all right, Ly?" Kate asks.

Kate, Lyla's legal guardian since their father died of a heart attack two years ago, is always looking out for us.

Lyla and Kate's mother lost her battle with cancer when Lyla was only two. She barely remembers her and though she misses her, Lyla's never lacked a motherly figure. Kate more than made up for any loss Lyla might have felt, and when my mother died, Kate stepped in and filled as much of that void as she could.

Part of me wonders if Jay will just blurt it out, tell everyone what I'd told him. Will I feel relief? Or will I only feel restraints when the people in white coats come to take me away?

Getting Jay to believe me was one thing, but convincing Kate and my father won't be so easy. Jay was convinced by the dirt I had on him. There isn't anything about Kate or my father that only I know.

Jay and I sit next to each other and across from my dad and Kate.

"Lyla, did you hear me?" Kate's voice interrupts my thoughts.

"Sorry, what?"

"I asked if you were okay?"

"Oh, um, yeah, I guess." I trip over the words, unsure exactly if I sound enough like Lyla. If I can't come clean, I'm going to have to try and pretend to be her, at least for a little while.

Kate rises from the chair. "We should go home."

No! Leaving the hospital, leaving my body is not an option. What if they cremate it? I blurt out, "I don't want to go. I can't leave."

I look to Jay, pleading with him to help me. I can tell he understands my panic, but that he doesn't know what to do.

"C'mon," he pauses and then forces out, "Lyla." Jay puts his hand on my shoulder. "It'll be okay."

"No, Jay, I can't leave. I need to stay. What if they … " I can't make myself say the word *cremate* out loud, though I am screaming it in my head.

They'll think I'm crazy, that I'm acting hysterical, but I have to do something. Racing toward my father, I kneel in front of his chair. "Don't cremate the body. Please, Mr. Clare, please. You can't. You can't."

He lifts me from the ground and wraps his arms around me. "Lyla, honey, everything will be fine." I clutch him, inhaling his familiar scent.

"Excuse me," a deep voice booms. We all turn. A husky police officer stands a few feet away. "Pardon the interruption, folks. I'm Officer Davies. I'm here to take your statement."

He is looking right at me. At Lyla.

"Do you mind answering a few questions for me? I promise not to take up much of your time." He ushers me away from my father, from the warmth. Icy chills pelt my skin. Folding my arms does nothing to steady the shivering.

Expressions of concern mixed with fear show on the faces of Kate, Jay, and my dad. They linger, unsure if they should sit, stand, or leave the room. I flash Jay a look that tells him to not leave me alone with the cops.

A female officer accompanies Officer Davies. She wears

a navy pinstripe suit and ill-fitting loafers. I think of Lyla and how she would disapprove of the boxy, scuffed shoes.

I follow the officers to the corner of the room and sit when they do.

"Spell your full name for me please," requests Officer Davies.

"L-y-l-a M-c-C-r-i-m-o-n-s." He scribbles in a small, worn, leather notebook as I speak.

My father, Jay, and Kate sit opposite us, far enough away that they can still listen in without being too obvious.

"Can you describe for me what you saw tonight? You were having a party?" Officer Davies prods me to start talking.

"Birthday party. For Mercy." Speaking of myself in the third person is beyond awkward.

"Do you know why she was in the alley?"

Yes, I *did* know why. I'd gone out to get some air. But I hadn't told that to Lyla, so I shook my head.

"Why were you in the alley?"

I tell him what I think is the truth, that Lyla went outside to look for me.

"Was this before or after the gunshot?"

My father gasps. Apparently he'd been unaware of what'd happened.

"Ms. McCrimons?" Officer Davies is anxious for my answer.

"Huh?"

"I asked you if you arrived in the alley before or after the gunshot."

"Before." It came out like a question.

"Did you see Mr. Andreas pull the trigger?"

Oh God! What do I tell him? I have no idea what Lyla saw.

Hesitating, I look to Jay.

Jay rescues me. "No, we didn't." Officer Davies looks irritated at first, but he lets Jay continue. "We couldn't see because Gage was directly in front of us. Then Mr. Andreas …" Jay pauses, swallowing. "Then we saw him fall."

The memory of it all comes flooding back: Mr. Andreas pointing the gun right at Gage. That's when I closed my eyes. I didn't want to see Gage get shot. But Mr. Andreas didn't shoot Gage. He shot himself.

"Was Mr. Andreas the only one with a weapon?" This time the female officer spoke. Her voice was lighter than I expected, but it wasn't anything close to friendly.

I look to Jay, hoping he'll answer again. He does. "Yeah."

Mr. Andreas pinned me up against the wall and wouldn't let me go. I tried to get away from him, but he was strong, surprisingly strong.

I didn't know Gage was there until he yelled.

They exchanged some words, like they knew each other. That part was confusing.

Mr. Andreas leaned into me and said, "I don't have much time. I've been searching for you, Mercy. I have so much to teach you about who you are." Then he shoved back from me and I fell.

While I tried to stand, Mr. Andreas pulled out a gun. I closed my eyes and covered my ears, trying not to scream.

The loud pop was deafening. I expected Gage to drop dead on the pavement, but instead it was Mr. Andreas that quivered to the ground, the butt of the gun protruding from his mouth. Blood ran from his nose and ears. Bits of brain matter splattered the concrete like lumpy strawberry jam colored confetti.

Gage blocked my path. At the same moment, the ground

was yanked from beneath me. Gage tried to catch me as I fell, but I went down too quickly. My knees and palms were scratched and bleeding, but that was the least of my problems. I seized and convulsed on the ground as what felt like thousands of bolts of electricity coursed through me.

Then, everything went black.

Chapter Eight

From her breast pocket, the female officer withdraws a Moleskine notebook. "We'll need to interview Gage as well. What is his last name?"

Jay and I look at each other. We don't know. "Um, we just met him. Today. He's new," I say.

Come to think of it, there isn't much I know about Gage. He helped me out earlier in the day and, after some arm-twisting by Lyla, agreed to be my date for the party. But he wasn't exactly the chatty type. At first, I thought he was just shy, but now I'm not so sure.

Officer Davies scans the room. "He's here at the hospital with you?"

"I haven't seen him around," Jay answers.

Where is Gage? He saves me from Mr. Andreas and then he just disappears? Something doesn't add up.

The two officers exchange a look that says they too think

it's strange that Gage isn't at the hospital. Do they suspect him of something? Gage is innocent in all this, as much a victim as I am. Right?

Officer Davies hands me a card, "If you hear from him you'll give us a call." This is a command, not a request. I nod and take the card.

Both officers stand. The woman adjusts her suit jacket. Before departing she says, "Do you know anything about the relationship between Mercy and Mr. Andreas? Why he was at the party?" There is an implication, a suggestion in her tone that makes me feel sick to my stomach.

"Mr. Andreas is a regular at Wally's," Kate says in a biting tone. "I seriously doubt he came for the party."

I more than appreciate Kate stepping in for me, trying to silence the idea that there is any relationship between Mr. Andreas and me. Never in a million years would I or Lyla, or anyone for that matter, have invited him to the party.

"I guess we'll never know," the detective says in a condescending tone.

"Mr. Andreas attacked me in that alley!" The words are out before I could stop them.

The entire room turns my way. Officer Davies is about to say something, but I cut him off.

"Not me, Mercy. He attacked Mercy." *Shut up! Shut up! Shut up!* I scream at myself. *You're making things worse.*

Both officers write in their notebooks. "Care to explain?" The female officer narrows her gaze until it zeroes in on me.

"That's what Gage told me," I lie. "He said Mr. Andreas grabbed Mercy and that he wouldn't let her go. Gage was trying to help her."

From deep within a tiny fire starts to grow. It licks at my

insides, spurring me forward. I stand and meet the female officer face to face. "I don't know what you think you know about Mercy, or Gage, or Mr. Andreas so let me tell you what I know. Tonight was supposed to be, my—" I stop, correcting myself, "—my best friend's birthday party. Gage did nothing wrong and neither did Mercy. And if you're trying to turn this into something else, well, that's just pathetic." In the corner of my vision I see the worried looks on Kate's, Jay's, and my dad's faces. They're wondering what's come over me.

I keep on. "Mr. Andreas shot himself and none of us know why. All we know is that it wasn't our fault, not mine, not Mercy's and not Gage's. You took our statements." Though I could hear myself talking, I don't know where the words come from. I'm not usually this provocative, this confrontational. "Now get out and let us grieve. Our friend died tonight. That's all that matters."

My rant over, I brace myself for the repercussions, but the two officers remain quiet for several moments. Finally, Officer Davies mumbles something about his sorrow for our loss and then they leave.

The rush of adrenaline passes, and I sink back into the chair and try to catch my breath. Whatever strength I'd felt before fades and the reality that I'd just yelled at two police officers sets in. This behavior is not mine. I am never this brave.

But Lyla is. This is exactly the kind of thing she'd say and do. She has bravado to spare, something I'd always admired and envied slightly about her.

"Holy shit, Lyla." Kate comes toward me, pulls me from the chair, and wraps me in a hug. "One of these days that mouth of yours is going to get you into serious trouble."

"Sorry, I couldn't help it," I tell her.

"We should go." Kate rubs my back one last time and then releases me from her grasp.

Somehow, despite all my fear, despite all my sadness, I am going to have to leave the hospital. I am going to have to leave my body behind.

"Can we do anything for you before we go, Eric?" Kate asks my dad.

My dad. There was only one other time I'd seen him look this way. The night my mother died. Then, just like now, there was a hollowness to his expression, like he was floating above, not quite connected to the tangible world. Then, he'd come back. He had to. For me. But now, there's nothing keeping him from the abyss. If he wants, he can completely succumb to the emptiness and let it take him.

There are so many things I want to say to him. But it would be strange for Lyla to tell him that she loves him or that he's a great father, so I keep quiet.

As if Jay can sense all that I'm thinking, he casually slides his fingers through mine and gives my hand a little squeeze. I squeeze back.

My father never answers Kate, so she rubs his shoulder and says good-bye and that she'll check in with him soon. Kate, so much younger than my father, is his equal when it comes to parenting. She seems to know exactly what to do, what to say, as if she's been given a manual to follow. Up until that moment I'd completely taken for granted that, like my father, Kate has lost everyone in her life. She just doesn't know it yet.

The walk to the car is quiet. Kate starts the engine while Jay and I say our good-byes.

I hook my thumbs into the belt loop of Lyla's jeans. Jay's hands are shoved into his back pockets.

"This isn't right," I say.

"What do you mean?"

"Look at us. We look completely uncomfortable."

"You sound like you. I think that's what's tripping me out the most. I mean the voice is Lyla's, but the expression, the way you say things, it's all you."

"Thank you for believing me."

"Mercy, what are we gonna do? I mean you can't just … what I mean is … "

"I can't pretend to be her forever, I know." Shame and guilt nearly suffocate me.

"Do you want me to come over?"

Jay's question catches me off guard. "Um, I don't know. Should I?"

"I think that's what Lyla would want, but if you don't … " He shrugs. "I don't know."

"Actually, I'd rather not be alone. I just didn't want to ask because, well, you know why."

Jay smiles with only the right side of his mouth. "I'm not mad at you, Mercy. I know this isn't your fault. I'm right behind you." A wave of relief washes over me.

I watch Jay jog off to his car before I open the door and climb in beside Kate. She and I had been alone together plenty of times before, but this time I am overly aware of myself. Am I sitting like Lyla, moving like she would?

"I can't believe she's really gone," Kate whispers. "It seems unreal, you know?"

"Yeah," is all I say in return.

The drive isn't too long, but it does include a trek along the freeway. Familiar street signs signal we are only five or six miles from home. Countless times I've driven this route going back and forth with Lyla to the mall. Multitudes of memories come back to me. The In and Out Burger which Lyla and I frequent nearly every day, always stopping for fries after school.

Jay would meet us there, too, and man, can he eat. It was like an event for him, as if he'd just made weight for an upcoming wrestling match. He'd order two double cheeseburgers, fries, and a fountain of Mountain Dew. Lyla and I would sit across from him, noses wrinkled in disgust as we watched him inhale the entire meal. How he didn't throw it all up later I'll never know.

Lyla and I are also regulars at Mimi's Boutique, which is located across the way from In and Out. You know you spend too much money at a store when every sales clerk knows you by name. Most everyone knows Lyla. She's a walking advertisement for Mimi's, though she also loves Forever 21 and H&M.

I shop at these places too, but Lyla never approves of my choices. While she opts for short shorts and skin-tight dresses, I gravitate more toward jeans and tank tops. Every once in a while I'll throw in a skirt just to mix things up and each time Lyla will pretend to faint. When she's finished teasing me, she always tells me how awesome I look, how beautiful I am, and that I shouldn't be afraid to show myself off a bit.

Who will say those things to me now? *Lyla? Where are you?*

Chapter Nine

Gage

R ae pulls the car behind the warehouse. Zee is waiting for us, arms folded across his chest, feet shoulder width apart. His usual stance.

"You know, I half thought she was kidding," he says to me.

"Is the room ready?" I ask him.

Rae climbs out of the car and slams the door. "I can't believe we're doing this."

"Zee, is the room ready?" I ask again.

He nods his shaved head. "Took some convincing, but Jinx came through."

Gingerly, I pull Mercy's body from the backseat of the car. With Zee's help, I cradle her in my arms and set off inside the building.

The halls are dimly lit, but nothing about that is unusual. We prefer to keep a low profile. I pass Jinx and the Observation Deck. He shakes his head at the sight of us and falls in step with the others behind me.

At the end of the hall, I push open a door and find what I'm looking for. Jinx has set up a hospital bed, one that we most often used for Breachers whom we need to keep medicated during interrogations. Next to the bed are the same monitors and machines that had been in Mercy's hospital room.

"I'll start the IV," Rae offers. As our resident intern, Rae handles all fluids and needles.

"Show me how," I say. "I can do it."

"Move." Rae shoves me aside. She works a needle into Mercy's arm and covers it with tape.

"What are you giving her?" I ask.

"What she needs," Rae answers.

Jinx stands in the corner, his hands clasped behind him. It's difficult to take Jinx seriously when he's angry because of his appearance. He has a full head of crazy curls that border on an afro, with a long, wide nose, and stubble that seems to be etched permanently into his face. Jinx is the character of the group, the jokester. But at the moment, there's no levity to his mood.

"Just say it, Jinx. I can feel your disapproval."

"What's the plan here, Gage? Help me understand." He strides toward the bed. "It looks like you stole the body of a Breacher and are planning to keep it alive. What I don't understand is why."

"Mercy," I say her name. She isn't an *it*. "Her name is Mercy."

"You see what I mean," Rae says to Jinx. "He's gone off the deep end with this one."

"Nathaniel had the chance to kill her and he didn't," I tell them. "He's been watching her for over a year. He wants something from her and we need to figure out what that is."

"Look, buddy," Zee says as he steps closer to me. "This has gone on too long. Nathaniel is getting to you. He's in your head. We can all see it."

I whip around. "He's not in my head."

"He is, man," Zee puts his hand on my shoulder. "Look what you're doing. You've stolen a body. For what? What could you possibly hope to gain from … " His voice trails off as a look of recognition spreads across his face. "No."

"Zee, hear me out," I try, but he cuts me off.

"No, Gage, you're crazy."

"What? What's going on?" Rae asks impatiently.

"Don't," I plead with Zee.

He ignores my request and turns to Rae and Jinx. "He's gonna try and put her back."

The look of dismay on their faces is unmistakable. My shame seeps from my pores and clogs the room. Zee is right. Putting Mercy back in her body is part of my plan.

"Gage! No!" Rae yells.

Jinx runs his hands through his tangle of hair. "You've got to be kidding me."

"Look!" I shout. "All of you! I can handle this. Everything is under control."

Zee balls his hands into fists and slides them into the pockets of his brown leather jacket. "Everything is not under control. You've gone too far. You're not thinking clearly."

"I am!" I stop myself, breathing deeply to steady my shaking hands. "I know this sounds crazy and I know you don't want to believe me, but I have to try and help her. I need to know what Nathaniel wants from her. Why shouldn't she go back? She's not like the others."

Rae rolls her eyes.

"That's not your choice to make, Gage," Jinx scolds me. "The Assembled set the rules."

Jinx is right. It isn't up to me. By bringing Mercy's body here I am putting all of them in danger. Maybe I'm asking too much of them.

I speak calmly when I say, "If any of you want out, I understand. And I won't hold it against you if you walk away. I know what I'm asking and I know what you're risking. You don't need to be on this ledge with me."

I take Mercy's lifeless hand in mine and stroke her cool skin with my thumb. "I've been fighting Nathaniel my entire life. And maybe you're right; maybe I'm letting it get to me, I don't know. But what I do know is that Mercy is a victim in this. She is whether you want to believe me or not. And I can't explain why, but I know I have to help her. If I do, I know it'll be the end of Nathaniel. I can feel it."

The room is dead silent as Rae, Jinx, and Zee consider my words. Rae gnaws her lip, sucking it between her teeth. I know I've gotten to her, but I don't know if it's enough for her to help me.

"I'm in." Zee grasps the rails of the bed. "I think you're crazy, but I'm in."

Zee looks to Rae, who looks to Jinx. He shrugs. Whatever Rae says, Jinx will go along with it.

"Fine," she relents. "I'm in too."

"One for all and all that other shit," Jinx adds.

"Thank you. All of you. I won't forget this."

"Don't worry, man." Zee claps his hand against my shoulder blades. "We won't let you."

"I have to find Mercy," I tell them. "Rae, you'll stay with her body?"

"Just call me Nurse Ratched," she quips.

"Rae," I glare at her.

"Fine. Florence Nightingale. Better?"

"Much." I turn to Jinx. "Get back to the OD and see about finding Nathaniel." Jinx nods and sets off to the Observation Deck.

"And me, boss? What can I do?" Zee asks.

"You can lend me some wheels," I tell him.

"Not the bike!" Zee roars.

I back out of the room, arms thrown up in surrender. "I'll bring her home safe and sound. I swear."

I spin on my heels and run, but not before I hear Zee yell one last time, "Not the bike!"

Chapter Ten

Zee's Ducati is parked in the back of the warehouse. His prized possession, he wipes "Fiona" down every day with a cloth diaper. I've never been much into motorcycles, but there is something very powerful about a Ducati and right now it's exactly what I need to get me to Lyla's house.

As I race through the streets all I can think about is Mercy. By now she is probably freaked out of her mind. I have a strong suspicion that I'm going to make her feel worse before it gets any better.

The Ducati roars one last time and comes to a stop at the end of Lyla's drive. Cutting the engine, I roll the bike up the path and park it, careful to make as little noise as possible.

Lyla's bedroom is around back. This I know from my surveillance of Mercy. Noiselessly, I let myself through the side gate. When I find the window I'm looking for, I knock. When nothing happens, I knock louder.

Finally a light flickers on and the window shade goes up. Mercy, or rather, Mercy in Lyla's body, stares back at me.

"Gage?" Her voice is muffled through the glass.

"I need to talk to you," I say and point toward the room, hoping she'll let me in.

She nods and slides the window open. I help her pop the screen off, and then I climb inside.

"The police are looking for you," she tells me.

"You were sleeping?" I say to her.

"I must've passed out. I don't remember." She comes fully awake then. "Jay!" She runs from the room leaving me standing alone in Lyla's bedroom.

The room is chaotic at best. Clothes strewn everywhere. A pile begins to move. The long tail of a black cat swishes against the floor and settles in. Careful not to step on it, I move around the room carefully.

Lyla is a girl who likes fashion models and boy bands. Every surface is covered in make-up and jewelry. The ceiling is plastered with glow-in-the-dark stars.

"He's asleep on the couch. Jay, that is," Mercy says when she comes back. She is still wearing street clothes, jeans, and a t-shirt.

"Do you want to talk here or go outside?" I offer.

"Outside. I don't want to wake anyone." She shuffles over to the closet. "Let me just grab a jacket."

On the chair behind me, half buried in a pile is a black hooded sweatshirt.

I hold it out to her. "Will this work?"

"Yeah, thanks."

We tiptoe down the hall and out the back door. The yard isn't much to speak of, mostly crab grass that desperately needs to be sheared and a few neglected potted plants. Mercy leads me to a weathered picnic table and set of chairs.

Silence passes between us. The entire ride over I planned what I was going to say, but being in front of her now, the words won't come.

"You said you wanted to talk?" she prompts me.

"I don't know where to start. I thought I would, but now I'm not so sure."

She half smiles at me, like she understands what it's like to be tongue-tied. I can't believe it. Here she is having the worst night ever and she's trying to put me at ease.

I decide to get straight to the bottom of it. "I know you're not Lyla," I tell her.

She snaps to attention; her entire body going rigid.

"I know that's you, Mercy. Inside Lyla's body."

"How do you know?" she whispers, her voice faltering with each syllable.

"I'm going to explain everything to you, but I need you to stay calm. Can you do that?"

She nods, but doesn't speak.

"I'm a Hunter, Mercy. I track Breachers."

Unable to comprehend, her brow furrows, nearly knitting her eyebrows together. "Breachers? What's a Breacher?"

"A Breacher is someone who lives eternally, able to jump from one body to the next."

"Okay, but what does this have to do with me?" she asks.

I take a deep breath. Time to stop dancing around and just say it. "You're a Breacher, Mercy. That's how you were able to take Lyla's body."

"Oh, my God." She leans back into the chair. "Why? Why am I like this?"

"Breaching is like a genetic trait, it's passed from one generation to the next," I explain.

Her eyes shoot open. "Wait. What are you saying?"

"I'm saying you are a Breacher, Mercy. Just like your mother."

Her mouth hangs agape as a quick puff of air escapes. Fear, hurt, anger, confusion, her expression says it all. She shakes her head. "That's not possible."

"I know this is difficult, but I'm telling you the truth."

"Do you know how crazy this sounds?"

"There's more." With my elbows on the table I lean closer to her. "You're in danger."

"What do you mean?"

"What happened tonight in the alley, that wasn't Mr. Andreas. That was Nathaniel Black. He's another Breacher. A very powerful one."

She lowers her head and pulls her knees to her chest. "This isn't happening."

"I know this is a lot, but I'll help you. You can trust me."

A flicker of anger flashes in her eyes. "How long have you known about me? About my mother?"

"Mercy."

She slams the chair to the ground as she gets to her feet. "You've known all along haven't you? You didn't just run into me at school today. You came looking for me." Her anger morphs into rage as she pieces things together. "Why didn't you tell me?"

"You need to calm down."

"Did you know I was going to die?"

I try to think of what to say, but she reads my expression too quickly.

"Oh. My. God. You did! You let me die."

"Please, Mercy. Let me explain." I reach out for her arm, but she yanks it away.

"Stay away from me. I mean it. I don't ever want to see you again! Go back to whatever hell you came from and forget you know my name!"

Chapter Eleven

Mercy

I slam the door behind me.

"Mercy!" Gage tries the handle, but I remembered to lock it. "Please, Mercy. Open the door."

"I said leave me alone!" Sinking to the floor, I try to catch my breath.

There is no way I am going to believe Gage. He is clearly a crazy person. But at the same time, some of what he said rings true. I'm not dead like I'm supposed to be. My body may have died, but I'm here, trapped inside Lyla.

I have more questions to ask him, too. Like what happened to Lyla? Am I stuck this way forever or can I get out? And if I do get out what happens to me? What happens to Lyla's body?

My head aches and my thoughts overwhelm me. I can't help the tears. Earlier I thought I only had to mourn the loss of my body, but now there is so much more. Nothing I thought about my life is real. It's all a lie. My mother isn't the person I thought she was. She wasn't even human. How am I supposed to deal with that?

Gage knocks lightly on the door. Part of me wants to ignore him, but the rest of me knows that I need him. He's the only one with answers. I dust myself off and open the door.

He follows me down the hall to Lyla's room and stands across from me while I climb onto Lyla's bed. I hug a pillow and sit cross-legged. It's a few moments before he speaks.

"I'm sorry." His voice is barely audible.

"I don't care."

Gage flexes his hands and takes a deep breath. "I need you to come with me. It's not safe for you here."

Involuntarily, my head moves back and forth. My body reacts before my mind has time to formulate and speak the words. "I can't go with you. I can't leave."

Both Kate and Jay appear in the doorway at the same time.

Kate looks from me to Gage and back again, suspicion rendering on her face. "What's going on?"

Jay rubs the sleep from his eyes. I want to tell them both what's going on, but now is not the time. I barely understand what Gage is trying to tell me. There's no way I can explain things to Kate and Jay.

"He heard about Mercy and he came to check on me," I lie. "He was just leaving."

Gage looks like he wants to protest, but I don't give him the chance. I cross the room and stand by Jay. Gage hesitates at first, but after a few seconds he relents. It's only when I hear the front door open and close that I finally exhale.

"I'm going back to bed," Kate says and then she leaves the room.

Jay hovers by the door looking unsure of what to do or say.

Still stunned, I don't know what to say to him either.

"Pancakes?" he asks.

Laughter escapes me. "What?"

"It's what I do for Lyla, when she's upset or doesn't feel well. I make her pancakes."

Right. I knew that. "Um, sure," I tell him. "But, Jay you don't have to, I mean, I'm not ... " I can't finish my sentence.

He finishes it for me. "You're not her, I know. But I have to do something."

"Okay."

I understand his need to do something because I have the same feeling. Things are so unsettled that anything routine, even if it isn't *my* routine, sounds heavenly. I go about straightening things up. My hands need to work; my brain needs to focus on a task in order to keep it from focusing on Breachers and Hunters.

I pick up some of the dirty laundry and throw it into the hamper. I have to shove it in because the hamper is already full. Lyla's closet looks like it has vomited by the way the shoes and belts and clothes spew forth.

I rack the shoes, hang the clothes, and roll up the belts. I tackle the scarves and other accessories next. It takes a while, but I make a dent in the mess. A few pieces of her furniture even have visible surfaces. Instead of making the bed, I strip it and throw the sheets into the wash. Doing so reminds me of a time, a few years ago, when Lyla and I were hanging out in her room on a random Friday afternoon. Somehow, we started talking about death. Between the two of us we have more knowledge of the subject than most.

"Do you think when you die you get to come back at all?" Lyla popped a handful of Skittles into her mouth.

"You mean like reincarnation?"

"No, not like that. I mean do you think you get to like go to your own funeral?"

"I don't think I'd want to go to my own funeral."

"Really?" Lyla scarfed down a few more pieces of candy. "I would. I mean, don't you want to see who turns out to mourn you?"

At the time I had a huge, albeit secret, crush on this guy in our class so I pictured myself dead and him standing by my casket. Maybe he'd lay a rose on top and tell me that he regretted never telling me how much he really liked me.

"Okay. I can kind of see your point," I admitted to Lyla. "But mostly, I think it would just be too sad."

"Why?"

"Because you'd be dead."

"Yeah, but what if you, like, got to haunt people. I'd totally haunt Jay."

"Jay?"

"Um, hello? I wouldn't want him to start hooking up with anyone else."

I threw a pillow at her. "You're nuts, Ly. You know that right?"

"And that's why you love me."

I did love her. I do love her. And I'm worried about her. I've been so caught up in my own drama that I forgot to ask Gage about Lyla. There are so many things that I still don't know about breaching, about my mother.

Jay calls from the kitchen letting me know breakfast is ready. Happy for another distraction, I curl my legs underneath me as I sit at the kitchen table.

Shaking his head, Jay laughs at me.

"What's so funny?"

He hands me a plate loaded with pancakes. "Lyla would never sit like that." He sits in the chair across from me.

Uncurling myself, I sit with my feet on the floor. "This feels weird."

"You're telling me."

We eat in silence for a few seconds before he starts laughing at me again.

"What now?"

"You cut your pancakes one bite at a time."

"Yeah, so?"

"Lyla always cut hers into tiny pieces, remember?"

I do remember. "And then she eats the middle piece first. She always says that's the way her dad served them to her, with the middle piece missing."

"Exactly."

Our enjoyment quickly fades. It's really starting to sink in that Lyla is gone and I am doing a horrible job impersonating her.

My fork drops against the plate. "I'm sorry. I suck at this."

"I can help, I guess."

This must be horrible for him. His girlfriend's body is seated across from him, but she isn't in it. Not even my imagination could reason with how strange it must feel.

"I'm sorry." I don't know what else to say.

"What did Gage really want?"

His abrupt subject change catches me off guard. A piece of pancake sticks to the back of my throat and I cough. Jay goes to the fridge, pulls out the orange juice, and pours me a glass.

When I stop coughing, I say, "Thank you." I wipe my mouth with a napkin and add, "You heard us?"

Jay set his fork down. "Not all of it. But enough."

Raking my hands though Lyla's thick dark hair, I knot my fingers at the back of my neck. "It's going to sound insane."

"I think we passed sanity about twelve hours ago," he quips, his lips pulling up at the edges into a shy smile.

"I can't even believe I'm going to tell you all of this. I mean, I'm not even sure if I believe it or understand or … "

"Mercy," he interrupts.

"I'm babbling like an idiot, I know. And Lyla never does that." Wadding up the napkin I throw it on the plate.

"What did Gage say?"

I figure there was no harm in just coming out with it. "He told me that I'm part of some freak species called Breachers that can live forever by jumping from body to body. Oh! And the best part, I apparently get this trait from my mother."

Jay's eyebrows are buried beneath his curls. If he tries to raise them any higher, they will disappear completely.

"Wow," he remarks.

"I know, right? It's insane. All of this is fucking insane."

"I, uh, I'm … " Jay stammers.

Echoing his sentiment of utter dismay I say, "Exactly."

Chapter Twelve

I send Jay home to shower and regroup. As much as I hate to see him go, we both need some time to process everything that has happened. It's not every day that your best friend dies, and later you find out that not only did she not die, but she took over your girlfriend's body because she isn't quite human, but rather some strange race of things called Breachers who can live forever by stealing bodies. It's a lot for Jay to take.

Once I suggested a shower to Jay I realize that I, too, am in desperate need. Kate and Lyla share a cramped bathroom full of mismatched towels. Over the toilet hangs a picture of a clown that Kate painted in elementary school. The counter is buried beneath makeup and varying lotions and crèmes in different stages of use ranging from nearly full to empty and expired.

Next to the sink are the toothpaste and two brushes: pink for Lyla, green for Kate. I've borrowed Lyla's stuff plenty of times, but using her toothbrush is kind of gross.

Her shower is not at all like mine. Low pressured and indecisive, the water fluctuates between damn hot and damn cold. I shower quickly, relieved to turn the water off at the end.

I need clothes so I have no choice but to go through her drawers. I try to ignore the fact that I have to wear her underwear. Today, like so many other days, it's going to be hot. Lyla has an array of skimpy clothing for just the occasion. It takes me a while to find something to wear given that Lyla and I don't exactly share the same taste in clothes. In the end I find a denim skirt that isn't of indecent length and the Train t-shirt I bought for her at their concert. I dig around in her closet until I find the pair of Keds I know she has shoved in there somewhere.

Doing Lyla's hair and makeup is quite the chore and I don't do it nearly as well as she does, but it's passable. Lyla is addicted to Sephora. She racks up more frequent buyer points than anyone. For my fifteenth birthday she bought me the entire Laura Mercier line complete with primers and blushes, brushes and eye shadows in what she called "neutral hues." All of it is still unwrapped and tucked neatly into the bottom drawer of my desk. It's not that I'm opposed to makeup. It's just that it takes so much time to do in the morning and I would rather sleep.

I find Kate at the kitchen table, reading the paper and drinking coffee. She looks tired, worn out. Rings of bluish purple circle her coal black eyes. Her hair, as dark as Lyla's, hangs in greasy strands around her face. She hasn't changed her clothes, still wearing the yoga pants and frayed sweatshirt from the night before.

Setting down her coffee she eyes me.

"What?" I ask, worried that I don't look enough like Lyla.

"I thought you hated Keds."

"Oh, I do. Mostly. But Mercy always wore them so, you know."

I hope she'll buy my explanation. When she reaches for her cup and takes another sip I figure she has.

"I need you to come to Wally's with me later. The place is still a mess from last night."

"Okay," I answer.

She eyes me again, "You're not going to give me shit about having to clean up?"

Damn! Lyla never agrees so quickly to clean up, mostly because Lyla never cleans anything up. Ever. "Oh, well, I just thought you probably really need my help." *Shit. Shit. Shit.* I sound nothing like Lyla. Kate will know something is up for sure.

"I don't think I've ever heard you offer to help me without some sort of bribe."

Thinking quickly I scowl at Kate. "Fine. God, if you're gonna be like this I can stay home. My friend just died you know? You could cut me some slack." This is exactly what Lyla would've said.

Kate shakes her head. Drinking the last of her coffee she pushes back from the table and stands. "I'm taking a shower. We'll leave in twenty." Before she leaves the room she turns and adds, "Your turn to take out the trash too, by the way."

I give her Lyla's best annoyed face. The roll of her eyes tells me I nailed it.

The trash can under the sink is filled to the brim. Carefully, I pull the red ties and cinch the bag closed without spilling any garbage on the kitchen floor. The bin is still on the curb so

I go out the front door. Crossing the lawn I meet with Lyla's neighbor. He waves.

It takes me a second to remember his name. "Hey, Mr. Sullivan." I wave back.

"I heard about your friend. Terrible news," he laments.

"Yeah."

"Do you have a sec? I think I got some of your mail by mistake."

"Um, actually—"

He cuts me off. "It won't take long. It's right inside."

"Okay." Dragging my feet, I follow him into the house. "Mr. Sullivan?" I say to the empty room.

Behind me, he closes the door. Startled, I whip around. "Sorry," I say, catching my breath. "I didn't see you there."

He turns the deadbolt. With the slow click of the lock he blocks the exit. Most of these homes are identical, so I know that I can make a run for it through the kitchen if needed.

"Why don't you have a seat? It'll just take me a minute to find that mail."

"Really, I have to go. My sister is waiting."

Mr. Sullivan leaps toward me. He thrusts his hands around my throat. I stagger, coughing and choking. He slams me into the wall. Stars fill my vision. Flailing, I try to pry open his grasp. This makes him squeeze tighter. Slowly, the room darkens.

Suddenly, Mr. Sullivan releases his grip and sinks to the floor. He clutches and claws at his back, but he can't reach the knife that's protruding from his skin.

My lungs burn for air.

"Did he hurt you?"

I hadn't noticed there was someone else in the room. He's

a severe looking man with defined cheekbones, deep set brown eyes, and a chiseled nose and chin. His dark hair is slicked and sharply cut.

"I don't think so." My voice is still weak.

Above Mr. Sullivan's body a black cloud rises. It swirls and eddies and finally morphs into a man. I stumble backward in a failed attempt to flee.

The severe-looking man rushes at the black cloud man and thrusts a tiny dagger into its heart. The black cloud man evaporates into wisps of smoky nothingness. The severe-looking man grins smugly.

Chapter Thirteen

"What the hell was that?" I choke out.

"That was me, saving your life."

I back away from him. "Who are you?"

"Nathaniel Black." The right corner of his mouth pulls into a grin, though it's more half smirk, half snarl. "Pleasure."

Stupefied, words are lost to me. Nathaniel Black: one of the most powerful Breachers. Nathaniel Black: the Breacher who killed Mr. Andreas. Nathaniel Black: the Breacher who is after me.

"Feel free to thank me." He rubs his hands together, clearly proud of himself.

Boldly, I fire, "You killed Mr. Andreas!"

Nathaniel shrugs and says, "Occupational hazard."

His arrogance and disregard for life spark an ember of disgust within me. "But in the alley, you attacked me."

"I had to get your attention."

"There are other ways to get someone's attention."

His lips pull up into a tight line. "Fear is a very effective attention getter."

"So by killing me, you were trying to get my attention?"

Nathaniel's expression changes dramatically. Gone is any semblance of the playful smart-ass he'd been as he charges toward me. Inches from me, he says in a low, guttural voice, "If I wanted to kill you, Mercy, you'd be dead."

Gulping, I inch backward. "Then what do you want with me?"

"I'm sure Gage already filled your head with all kinds of stories."

"He said you wouldn't stop until you get what you want."

Mr. Sullivan's body lies lifeless just a few feet from me. Blood pools beneath him, thick, nearly black, like sludge.

"Gage is not one of us, Mercy. It would be best if you remembered that."

"*He's* trying to help me."

"Wrong!" Nathaniel roars. "He's a Hunter, Mercy. His sole purpose is to find and slaughter Breachers."

My head spins. I don't know who to trust or what to believe, but judging from the dead body at my feet, Nathaniel isn't all that great of a guy. Before I can decide whom to believe, I have more questions.

"Who was that?" I gesture toward Mr. Sullivan's dead body.

Nathaniel nudges him with his toe. "That was one of Ariana's goons." Perceptive to my confused look, Nathaniel continues before I ask the obvious question. "Who's Ariana? Well, she's your mommy dearest."

My limbs go numb. "That's impossible," I spit. "My

mother is dead."

"In theory."

Needing to sit down, I lumber over to the couch and lower myself into the cushions. Leaning forward I put my head between my knees.

"Try not to vomit on the rug," Nathaniel says. "We wouldn't want to leave Lyla's DNA at a murder scene."

My second murder scene in less than twenty-four hours. This is not the kind of record I was hoping to set.

Nathaniel sits on the coffee table in front of me. Being so close to him ignites my skin to tingling. I can feel the electricity coursing through me and the air around me is full of static.

Learning my mother was a Breacher is one thing. But Gage didn't say anything about her still being alive. He'd lied to me by omission. My skin buzzes with the knowledge that if he lied to me about that, there's a chance he'd lied about other stuff too.

Nathaniel said that this thing, this Breacher inside of Mr. Sullivan, was one of Ariana's goons? If that was true, that meant that not only was she alive, but that she sent someone to kill me—her own daughter.

I look up at Nathaniel, too tired to fear him. I half say, half whimper, "He was trying to kill me."

"He was trying to kill this body," Nathaniel corrects me.

"I don't understand. Why would he want to kill Lyla?"

"Think of this more like a flesh suit." Nathaniel picks at my hair, Lyla's hair. "You're not much use to anyone inside of that thing."

Shivers of disgust ripple through me. To think that he could call Lyla, my best friend, a flesh suit is unacceptable.

"So you have no regard for human life at all? You think it's fine to go around killing people?"

"It's either them or me. Which would you choose?"

I fire the nastiest look I can muster. He eyes me sideways. "C'mon. You haven't at least thought about it?"

I turn my back to him. "I'm not going to talk about this with you."

"Why not? I'm the perfect person to discuss this little dilemma with."

Frustrated, I leave the couch. It's too much to be this close to him.

"You're a smart girl, Mercy. I know you've put the pieces together. If you want out of that body, you're going to have to kill it." He ends his sentence with a sing-song note.

The truth is finally laid out before me. When Gage told me that Breachers could live forever by jumping from body to body, I hadn't been strong enough or brave enough to ask him how. Maybe that's because I already knew. Somewhere deep inside, inherently, I knew. The only way to get out of Lyla's body is to kill it. For good.

I suppose it was stupid or naïve to think that when I left her body she would reappear as if nothing had ever happened. Regardless, that's what I'd hoped. I'd clung to the hope that maybe Lyla wasn't gone, just trapped even further inside herself, and that once I left she'd resurface.

"I can't kill my friend," I tell him.

"Then you'll live in her body forever. Either way, she's gone. You didn't die, Mercy." He comes around to face me. "She did. And the sooner you accept that, the better."

His words tear through my chest and I succumb to reality.

"I can't."

"You can."

Either choice is hell. Pretend to be her. Kill her.

"We should get out of here." Nathaniel takes my arm.

Yanking it away, I say, "I'm not going anywhere with you!"

"This won't be the last time she sends someone after you, Mercy. She'll keep coming."

"That's what Gage said about you," I remind him.

The expression on his face is a mixture of irritation and displeasure, as though my words sting.

"Fine. Let's see how far you get on your own."

Chapter Fourteen

Gage

Zee forgives me for taking the Ducati. I pay him off with a new stack of diapers and the special wax he always uses. I don't have the heart to tell him, or any of them, for that matter, that I'd failed. Mercy wouldn't listen to me. Not that I blame her exactly, but without being able to tell her everything about her mother, I left there feeling worse than ever.

I didn't intend to keep secrets from her. I was merely trying to dole out the bad news in small doses, not wanting to tell her anything I didn't think she was ready to handle. It was enough to learn that her mother was a Breacher. I didn't even know how to begin to tell her that her mother was the oldest, most feared, most dangerous and evil Breacher in creation.

I wander around the warehouse for a while, thinking, pacing, trying to come up with my next move. I know I need to give Mercy time to work things through, but how much time is enough time? If it were solely up to me, I'd be on my way back there now. I try to remember that Mercy's method of thinking is nothing like mine. She's half human, half Breacher, and that makes her emotional status questionable at best.

On my last lap through the warehouse I stop in the room set up for Mercy's body. It's dark and quiet except for the steady beep of the heart monitor. Her hair is losing its reddish sheen. The pink in her soft, round cheeks is nearly invisible. She's fading with each passing moment. A body without a soul cannot last for long.

Rae comes through the door and goes straight to the bags of fluid to check their levels without saying anything to me.

"It didn't go well," I tell her.

"What kills me, Gage, is that you expected it would." Rae's blond hair swishes across her dark blue shirt as she works, as golden bright as a surfer girl's. Her appearance is the exact opposite of her personality, which leans toward dark, brooding, and sullen. Her sapphire blue eyes rarely show any kindness behind them. Rae is hard, determined, and focused. She is a Hunter through and through.

"I wasn't able to tell her anything about Ariana. She threw me out before I had the chance."

Rae laughs. "At least the girl has some fight in her. She's going to need it."

"Tell me honestly, Rae. Do you think I'm doing the right thing by wanting to help her?"

Rae pauses, hooks a new bag to the IV line and turns to face me square on. "I think you're letting humanity creep in. I think your judgment is compromised. But if I was in your position, I might do the same thing."

"So you understand?"

"I understand that we do things we shouldn't or wouldn't

normally do for the people we love."

Her words surprise me. It's unlike Rae to ever talk this way. But it isn't just her mention of the word love that throws me off; it's the implication of her statement.

"You think I love her?"

She looks at me like I'm an idiot. It's a look I've come to know well.

"Gage, you know you do. We all know you do. You held out showing it for a long time, but I knew from the first time you looked at her."

She's right. But that doesn't mean I have to admit it out loud.

Rae lowers her eyes, fixating her gaze on the floor. "Gage, it's against the rules to love a human. You know it isn't going to end well." She tilts her head up and her eyes lock to mine. "So, stop. You aren't human, you don't have to give in to whatever it is your feeling. Get yourself in check, for all our sakes."

Patting my shoulder before she exits the room, Rae leaves me alone with Mercy's body, alone with my thoughts, and with the aching pit in my stomach that tells me she's right.

The sound of footsteps running down the hall breaks my contemplation. Jinx, holding onto the doorframe to steady himself, skids to a stop.

"We've got trouble."

Close on Jinx's heels, I run to the Observation Deck. Jinx slides back into his seat behind the controls, his hands working deftly as he uses the touch screen on the table to bring the board of monitors to life.

Usually split into multi-screen, picture-in-picture monitors of multiple locations at once, Jinx works until the board shows but one location: the house next door to Lyla's.

"What did you find?" I ask, my hands gripping the rails.

"We got a reading about ten minutes ago. Definite Breacher activity."

"Nathaniel?"

"Yeah. But not just him. Watch."

Jinx zooms in on the house and at first nothing happens. No heat source, no energy mass.

After a few seconds, not one, but two energies emerge on the screen, red and yellow blobs shaped as humans.

"What just happened?" I ask Jinx after one of the energies goes dark.

"Don't know. But look," he points. "The second energy remains for a while, maybe ten to fifteen minutes."

"How many humans?" I ask him.

"Two. One alive. One dead."

"I'm going over there," I tell him.

"Alone? Not a good plan, Gage. Take Zee with you."

"Tell him I'll call him if I need him."

Not wasting any time, I hustle across the warehouse to where I left the Ducati. Zee blocks my path.

"Uh-uh," he says. "No way. Not again."

"I need the bike, Zee."

"Do you remember crashing your car, Gage? How you wrapped that little beauty around a tree?"

My Mercedes. I remember the accident vividly. But that is beside the point.

"I brought the bike back safely last time, didn't I?"

"Yes. But that doesn't mean you're likely to do it again."

"Mercy could be in danger. Are you going to argue with me about your stupid bike, or are you going to get out of my way?"

His right eyebrow arches high on his forehead. Calling the bike, the one human possession Zee allowed himself to love, stupid, was not my smartest move.

"I'll drive." Rae's heeled boots clack across the floor. "Don't even bother trying to talk me out of it. I'm going."

There'd be no arguing with her. We head over to her car, a feisty, classic red Midget. We arrive at Lyla's house in no time.

I knock on the front door while Rae goes next door to investigate the scene. By the time she gets back to me, I'm still knocking.

"Jinx was right. One dead." She crosses the lawn. "It's not Mercy. Looks like the old guy who lived there."

I wipe my hand across my mouth. "I don't like this, Rae."

The look on her face tells me she doesn't like it either. Something is up and we have to find Mercy.

We creep around the side of the house and peer through the windows. It doesn't look as though anything is disturbed. It simply looks like they aren't home.

"What do you want to do?" Rae asks me.

I consider our options. We can go back to the warehouse and wait, but I'm too restless for that. The only real choice is to look for her. I'm not going to be able to sit still until I know she's safe.

I decide Rae and I should start from the beginning, that we should go back to the place where everything went horribly wrong.

"Let's go to Wally's," I say to Rae. "That's where the party was last night."

Rae drives through the city streets at breakneck speed. She's a much better driver than I, which is partly the reason I hadn't bothered to replace my car. With Rae at the wheel I can focus, keep my thoughts on Mercy instead of oncoming telephone polls.

Wally's looks different in the daylight. A few police cars and some crime scene investigation units are still on the scene. This means we're going to have to be discreet. The last thing I need is to spend hours in an interrogation room.

"Pull up to that corner," I tell Rae.

"You saw all the cops, Gage. It's probably better if you stay in the car."

"Are you offering to go talk to her?" I can't hide my surprise. "Tact isn't exactly a specialty of yours."

Rae turns the keys and shuts off the engine. "I will be a perfect angel."

Her tone is less than reassuring. "I think I'll risk it," I tell her.

Rae turns toward me and puts her hand on my knee. The warmth that radiates from her touch is both unsettling and calming all at the same time.

"Gage, let me help you. I can. And I want to."

She's cracked through my exterior and she knows it.

"I'll be back soon." She exits the car and walks toward Wally's leaving me to stew and worry.

Chapter Fifteen

Mercy

Wally's is a mess. The aftermath of the party makes it look like a confetti hurricane has blown through. The tables, pushed to the sides in order to make a dance floor, are covered in plates, cups, bottles, and all sorts of trash.

Kate works behind the bar, clearing and scrubbing and putting things back in order. She gives me the chore of sweeping the floor and putting the tables back in their usual places. Clearly, I drew the short stick. It's getting easier to understand why Lyla complained about working at Wally's all the time.

Trash bag in hand, I traipse around the room clearing the tables, deciding the floor will have to come last. Once the bag is bursting, I head out toward the alley to the dumpster.

My entire life changed in the alley. I just didn't know it at the time. Mr. Andreas's body is gone, but the blood spatter remains. An officer catches me staring and shoos me along.

"Mercy?"

A stunningly gorgeous girl saunters toward me. She moves with grace and purpose. Her blond hair has that beachy look, waves here and there and a ton of natural shine. It's the look Lyla is always trying to achieve. Lyla would've drooled over her wardrobe as well. Skinny jeans tucked into stiletto boots with a fitted tee and cropped jacket, she is just off the pages of a magazine.

I am so mesmerized by her appearance that it takes me a few seconds to realize that she called me Mercy. In my short time in Lyla's body only two people have known who I really am, and neither of those encounters went very well. Bracing myself for the worst, I nod to let her know that yes, I am Mercy.

I wait for her to speak.

"I'm Rae." She holds out her hand for me to shake. "I'm a friend of Gage's."

When I don't reciprocate the gesture she pulls her hand back and says, "Okay."

"What do you want?" I ask her.

She adjusts her stance, shifting from warm to put-off and annoyed. "I came here to help you," she tells me.

Get in line, I think. Gage's help nearly got me killed and Nathaniel's help left Lyla's neighbor dead. Unless this Rae girl has an exact plan of how to get me out of Lyla's body without having to kill her, I'm not interested in anything she has to offer.

"You don't want my help, do you?" She steps between me and the back entrance to Wally's. "I can understand that. And just between us girls," she leans in close, "I don't want to help you either. You are a soul-sucking Breacher and nothing would give me more pleasure than to end you right now."

Irritation takes a backseat to fear. My palms start to sweat.

"Relax," she continues. "I'm not going to kill you. Like I said, I'm here to help you."

"Why?"

"For Gage." She spins around and starts back down the alley toward the sidewalk. Just as she reaches it, she whirls back around and calls out, "Meet me tonight. Seven thirty, corner of 13th and J. I'll be waiting."

I watch her disappear around the corner. It's only when she is out of sight that I realize I'm trembling. She says she wants to help me. She says she's doing it for Gage. Can I trust her? I suppose I don't have much choice.

It's difficult to believe what my life has come to in less than twenty-four hours. I never should've let Lyla throw me a birthday party. I told her I didn't want one. Nothing good ever comes from celebrating my birthday. But I'd gone along with it because she was so determined to make the night special for me. It's not her fault things ended up the way they did. It's mine.

The guilt is crushing. But it isn't the only emotion nipping at me. There's plenty of anger and resentment in the mix and all of it is directed at my mother.

As far as I knew, my mother was Molly Sherman. She was a student at Sacramento City College when she met my father. He was the teaching assistant for her Introduction to Western Civilizations class. My dad told me how he was so taken with her that when he stood to greet her, he knocked over his cup of coffee, spilling it down the front of his pants. She'd burst out laughing. He couldn't help himself, he'd laughed too.

For their first date he'd taken her to see a revival of Psycho. It's not exactly the most romantic movie in the world, but she'd never seen it and my dad has a major thing for Hitchcock. They'd spent the entire movie huddled together sharing popcorn.

They'd married four years later on the anniversary of their first date. My mother had no family to speak of so they married in a small courthouse ceremony with only a judge and my paternal grandmother for a witness.

They hadn't taken a honeymoon, not in the traditional sense. There was no money for a Hawaiian vacation or anything like that, so my dad had created a paradise for her in the backyard. He'd set up Tiki torches and a picnic blanket. He'd special ordered a Hawaiian Lei from the local florist. They'd eaten barbecue and fresh fruit.

I was born ten months later. My mother had stayed home with me while my dad worked. She was the best. She took me to the park almost every day. She made cookies and hot chocolate. When I was sick, she made her famous chicken soup and sometimes she even slept on a chair next to my bed just in case I needed her during the night.

How could she not tell me who she really was, or who I really was for that matter? Why did she keep it from me?

"Ly, what're you doing out here?" Kate dries her hands off on a rag as she approaches.

I shake my head and start to cry. She folds me into her and holds me while I sob. Kate lets me get it all out, holding me tightly until the very last tear falls.

"What am I gonna do?"

"We'll get through this," she assures me. "Just like we've gotten through everything else. Together."

"I can't do it. It's too much." Just when I think the well of tears is dry, more come gushing forth.

"Hey," she says firmly. "You can't fall apart. You have to just keep going. One foot in front of the other."

It's her standard pep talk, one that I've heard plenty of times before whenever Lyla or I faced something difficult.

I need my dad. I need Lyla. I need someone to help me. All the things I want to say, but know that I can't, swim around my mouth and lodge there until I choke on them.

"Breathe, Ly. Try and calm down. This is the worst of it and it'll only get better," Kate tells me.

If she only knew how wrong she was.

Chapter Sixteen

For the next several hours I concentrate on the menial tasks at hand. I clear and wipe down tables. I sweep and mop the floor. I even clean the bathrooms. Putting Wally's back in order is all I think about until we finish. When Kate flips off the lights and we walk out, I worry that my mind will start to race and wander again.

Kate's cell phone rings once we get to the car. She grabs my hand, gives me a strange look, like she needs to take a moment, and then she answers the phone.

"Hi, Eric."

Dad! The ache for him is nearly overwhelming. It takes some strength not to yank the phone from Kate's hand just so I can hear his voice.

Kate nods along while he speaks and then she says, "Of course. We can do that. We'll be over soon. Okay. Bye."

"What did he say?" I ask.

"He wants us to help him pick out something for Mercy to wear."

"To wear?"

"For the burial."

"Oh."

The burial. At least he isn't going to cremate me. This did little to give me comfort. I am still dead. It seems wrong somehow that I should be asked to pick out my own burial outfit.

I force myself to think like Lyla would in this situation. If she were here, instead of me, she would take the task of selecting my last outfit very seriously.

When Kate and I get out of the car and stand on the sidewalk in front of my house, it seems neither of us is willing to take the first step.

"Ready?" Kate asks me.

"Nope."

She puts her hand on the small of my back, nudging me forward.

The house isn't much to speak of, but it's lovingly cared for. While my mother was around she kept house, spending her days cooking, cleaning and occasionally shopping. She made this house a home and, in her absence, my father and I did our best to maintain it.

The family room is cozy and comfortable, with Pottery Barn slouchy couches, a leather ottoman, and a set of matching recliners. Above the mantel hangs a family photo taken seven years ago. Books and newspapers are strewn about. Between my father and me, we have enough magazines to fill a doctor's office.

Beyond the living room and off to the left is a dining

room and a tiny kitchen. To the right are my father's office, a bathroom, and my room. My father's room is in the back left corner of the house. He keeps the door closed at all times.

When my dad answers the door it's obvious that he's been crying. He hugs us both and offers us something to drink, which we decline. Kate tells him we won't take too long. He profusely thanks us for helping him and we tell him that we're happy to help.

Kate follows me into my room. I stop about halfway in.

"You okay, Ly?" I shake my head no. "Me either," Kate agrees as she goes to the closet and flips through its contents.

"What are you looking for?" I ask her.

"Something … respectable, not flashy, and not entirely depressing."

"How do you know so much about this?" I asked her.

She looks at me for a second like she thinks I'm crazy and then she says, "Well, I have done this twice."

I'd forgotten. Kate has buried both of her parents. She's planned funerals and made arrangements. She knows all about this kind of thing.

I wander about, feeling strange to be in my room as an observer and not an occupant. I notice things about myself for the first time, like how all of the books on the second shelf of my bookcase start with the letter P. I don't remember doing that on purpose.

"How about this?" Kate holds up my tan skirt and white blouse. I do not want to be buried in that.

"Kinda boring, don't you think?"

"Okay, what about this?" Next she holds up a black dress that I've never worn. The price tags are still attached.

"I'd forgotten about that." I take the dress from Kate and

lay it across the bed.

Kate picks up the price tag. "I wonder why she never wore it."

"She was waiting for her first date." I'd never actually told Lyla that. Lyla didn't even know I had the dress because if I showed it to her she would've made me wear it and I wanted to save it for a special occasion. My funeral is not the special occasion I had in mind.

"I'm not sure we should bury her in black though," I say.

"Yeah, you're probably right." Kate grabs the hanger and puts the dress back in the closet.

"Let me look." It is, after all, my closet. I pull out a cream-colored sheath with a tiny gold belt around the middle. "This is good, right?"

"That's perfect. What about shoes?"

"Umm … " I search the floor. "These will work." I show her a pair of nude kitten heels, one of the only pair of high heels I own. If Lyla were here, she would've picked these out first and then picked a dress to match. Shoes are Lyla's specialty.

"I think we're done here then." Kate scans the room. "Are we really going to do this?" She looks to me for the answer, but I don't have one so I hug her until she pulls away.

Taking one last look around my room, I wonder if I'll ever see it again. Will my dad throw my stuff away or keep it a shrine like people do sometimes? It's tempting to take a few things with me, like my favorite USC t-shirt or the dried corsage from last year's father/daughter dance, but I leave them all, too afraid that if I take anything, I'll try and take everything.

Kate calls out to my dad as we leave my bedroom, "Eric."

"In the kitchen," he calls back.

He stands at the counter, looking out into the backyard. The sink is full of last night's dishes.

"We left the clothes on the bed," Kate tells him.

"Thank you."

We say our good-byes and I leave, knowing that the next time I see him it will be at my funeral.

Chapter Seventeen

Gage

"You need to stop pacing. You're making me dizzy." Rae glares at me.

"I hate waiting."

"No shit. She said she'd be here. Just relax."

I reach into my jacket pocket for my phone and press the home button. The screen lights up, letting me know it's seven forty-five PM. "She's fifteen minutes late."

"That doesn't mean anything other than she's late. Stop reading into everything."

"If only we could figure out what Nathaniel wants."

"Does it matter what he wants? She'll lead us to him, we'll kill him, and then it'll all be over."

"I don't like the idea of using Mercy as bait."

"Yeah, well, you're going to need to get over that."

I give Rae a dirty look.

"Fine." She throws up her hands. "We'll keep your precious

Mercy safe."

There's nothing in her tone that even remotely resembles sincerity. But before I have the chance to say anything, Mercy comes walking down the street toward us.

Her gait is steady, cautious. I can see that she's nervous and that she's trying to hide it. But she's here and that's a start. As much as I want to rush to her, I don't want to startle her, so I plant my feet and wait.

I hate waiting.

"Hey," Mercy says.

"Thanks for coming," I say. She nods. "It's this way."

I lead the way while Rae brings up the rear. It isn't my intention to flank Mercy; it just sort of happens that way. From the way she keeps looking over her shoulder at Rae, while I keep looking over my shoulder at her, it's a wonder that neither of us walks headfirst into a street lamp.

The entrance to the warehouse is nondescript, just another door on what appears to be an abandoned building. It isn't until we get into the entryway that it's possible to notice that this is no ordinary warehouse.

The keypad on the wall to my left flips open at my touch. I type in the code and lean forward to allow for the facial recognition test. Once I'm cleared, the inner door slides open allowing us to pass.

I step aside as Rae leads Mercy through the entrance and into the warehouse. Mercy looks around, taking everything in, but she doesn't comment. Zee and Jinx are waiting for us at the Observation Desk.

Mercy tries, but she can't hide her reaction the O.D.. Her eyes are as big as saucers.

"What is this place?" she asks.

"This is my baby," Jinx speaks up. "Pretty awesome, don't you think? We're wired into every network, every surveillance system. It's our window to the world."

"So you're spying on everyone?"

"We're protecting everyone," Rae says sharply. "From Breachers like you."

"Nice work," Mercy shoots back while she gestures toward Lyla's body.

"Breachers give off a different energy," Jinx continues. "Like a heat source. That's how we know where they are."

"Then you know about Mr. Sullivan and that Nathaniel Black guy. You could see it?" Mercy asks Jinx.

He answers, "Not exactly."

"We can see the energy, but that doesn't identify the specific Breacher," I tell her. "So, it was Nathaniel?"

Mercy keeps watching the multi-screen projection while she speaks. "Mr. Sullivan said he had our mail. As soon as I got inside his house I knew something was wrong, but I didn't act. It's like I talked myself out of it or something." She pauses, pushing a strand of hair behind her ear. "Then he grabbed for my throat and I couldn't breathe."

"I'm sorry," I say, putting my hand on her shoulder. I expect her to shrug me off, but she doesn't.

"I thought I was going to die, again," she whispers. "I don't know where Nathaniel came from or how he got there. He was just there. And he killed Mr. Sullivan and that's when things got weird. Or *weirder*, I guess."

Slowly, so as not to scare her, I remove my hand from her shoulder. "Can you describe it for us?"

"I'm not even sure what I saw. It was like this black fog or cloud or something. And it looked like it might be a man, but I couldn't really tell. It didn't last long."

"What do you mean?" I ask her.

She looks up at me when she says, "Nathaniel had a knife and he stabbed him or it, or whatever, and then it was gone."

Rae, Jinx, Zee, and I all exchange knowing looks. What goes unspoken between us is our heightened sense of uncertainty regarding Nathaniel. It's time to stop messing around and figure out what he's up to once and for all.

Though I don't like it, Rae is right. We need Mercy to get to him. Whether or not she's willing to cooperate is still up in the air.

"Are you going to tell me what's going on?" Mercy asks, interrupting my thoughts.

I look to Zee. "You want to take this?"

Zee steps forward and Mercy recoils. He's intimidating in stature, with the look of someone who shouldn't be messed with, but at heart Zee's a creature full of compassion and understanding. Fiercely loyal and brave, I've put my life in his hands on more than one occasion and I'd do it again without even thinking.

He bends at the waist just slightly, as if he's bowing, and says to Mercy, "If you'll just follow me this way, please."

Mercy looks to me for reassurance and with a slight nod of my head I signal to her that Zee can be trusted.

I follow them down the hall to the Records Room, the place where we keep and store all of our investigations. Zee is the Records Keeper, a librarian of sorts.

"Right through here." Zee opens the Records Room door.

We cross the threshold into a room that looks very much like a library. Long tables are capped with bookshelves that appear to stretch endlessly into the distance.

Zee pulls out a chair for Mercy at a table near the center of the room. He dims the lights with a remote control. With a few more clicks a large screen lights up the wall in front of us.

A row of people dressed in white robes appear on the screen.

"What is this?" Mercy asks.

"Nathaniel Black's sentencing. I thought you'd like to see for yourself exactly what we're up against," Zee explains to her.

"This is The Assembled," I point to the screen. "They're keepers of peace and they make sure that the human world stays safe."

We turn our attention back to the screen.

Samuel Maine, first assistant, speaks first, "Nathaniel Black, do you deny the charges brought against you by the High Council?"

Nathaniel, sharply dressed in a black suit, crisp silver shirt, and a matching silver tie, sits behind a large wooden table. His eyes shimmer in the fluorescent light, giving them an unnatural glow. When he smiles, his painfully white teeth flash wickedly. His hair is slicked back. He has the air of a smooth-talking used car salesman.

Judging from the way Mercy sinks deeper into the chair I can tell that she already knows exactly how dangerous Nathaniel is.

"Ladies and Gentlemen." Nathaniel rises from the chair with supreme arrogance. "May I approach?"

"Step lightly, Nathaniel," Samuel warns.

"Of course." When Nathaniel speaks, his voice oozes forth in a sweet, gooey, patronizing syrup.

He walks noiselessly to the center of the floor and turns

his back to The Assembled, choosing instead to face the pews before him, giving the illusion that he was speaking directly to us.

"My friends," he begins, "there is no crime here. I'm simply exercising my free will, a gift that cannot be withdrawn. The Assembled are not the source of such generosity. *He* alone bestowed this power upon me. And *He* alone," he turns slightly, shooting a quick glare at The Assembled behind him, "can take it away."

"You have abused your gift, Nathaniel," Margaret Start, third from the left snaps.

"Who's to say?"

"We are to say!" the head of The Assembled, Lucas Church, rises from his chair and shouts. "The crimes against you are heinous and you must suffer the consequences."

"Do you threaten me?" Nathaniel chuckles.

"Do you deny the charges against you?"

Nathaniel tilts his head to one side. "I do not."

"Then you shall be sentenced."

"You cannot punish me. I do not answer to you." Nathaniel's voice remains cool, not showing even the slightest agitation.

"You answer to the laws that govern us all and we are the body that enforces those laws," Lucas speaks with a grave tone.

"Fine." Nathaniel waves his hand dismissively. "Do what you must."

Lucas Church, followed by the others, stands. "Nathaniel Black, you are hereby sentenced to servitude on Earth. Since it seems you are so obsessed with human life, you shall become human."

Nathaniel halts dead in his tracks. He pivots abruptly. "You cannot lower such a sentence! You have no right!"

"You will live your life on Earth, Nathaniel," Lucas continues, ignoring Nathaniel's pleas. "You will live as a human and you will die as a human." The old man bangs a gavel. "Guards."

Three imposing shadows step forward. They wear service uniforms, much like that of military personnel.

"You can't do this to me!" Nathaniel screams as they restrain him. With great effort they bind him with chains.

"You'll regret this!" He continues to yell as they lead him from the room.

The screen fades. It's only then that I see Mercy exhale.

"Why are you showing me this?" she asks quietly.

"Patience." Zee clicks a different button on the remote control.

A hospital room shows on screen. An elderly man, obviously stricken with disease, lies in the bed. Tubes protrude from his arms, his mouth, and his nose. The machine behind him blips slowly, monitoring the faint beat of a weakening heart. A nurse enters the room, takes his pulse, and adjusts his covers. She checks the tubes and changes the bags of fluid. Before she has time to leave the room, the monitor's alarm sounds.

She takes the man's pulse again. Removing the stethoscope from around her neck, she listens to his heart. Another nurse comes into view. The beeping morphs to a flat line, which rings one continuous and final note.

"Call it," the second nurse says.

"Time of death, eleven thirty-one AM." She covers him with the sheet. "Rest peacefully, Mr. Black."

Mercy flinches every so slightly.

The second nurse leaves the room.

The first nurse goes about disconnecting wires, not noticing at all what is going on around her. Mercy edges forward in her seat, placing her hands on the table, her mouth hangs slightly agape.

Above the body a dark light hovers. Like a storm cloud it swirls furiously, slowly taking shape. The nurse turns around and finds herself face to face with the real Nathaniel Black. He isn't aged, wrinkled, or sickly. He's the same Nathaniel he'd been in the courtroom; the same creepy smile, the same devilish eyes. He checks himself over, as if admiring what he sees.

Then, quick as lightning, he lunges forward. I hear Mercy let out a tiny gasp as Nathaniel reaches for the unsuspecting woman's throat.

The nurse widens her mouth to scream, but it's too late. A low gurgling sound bubbles forth as he chokes her. Without warning, Nathaniel's grip on the woman loosens and he begins to shake uncontrollably. His victim's eyes widen, horrified.

Nathaniel's body shatters into a million pieces. Stunned, unable to run, the nurse stands there and watches as the pieces, like a swarm of bees, fly into her mouth. Then it's her turn to shake.

She writhes, buckling to the ground. Her body thrashes against the floor. Finally it stops and her body is still.

To the unknowing, she appears dead. But then she rises from the ground. She pauses, steadying herself against the bed. She looks up, as though she knows she's being watched. It's like she's looking right at the camera; her eyes are yellow and menacing. She stretches her neck, smoothes her clothes, and leaves the room.

The screen goes black. I can see Mercy's hands shaking

against the table. "As far as we know," Zee says. "That was the first recorded breach."

"But how? Why? I don't understand." She isn't talking to Zee or me. She's on the verge of uncontrollable babble.

With just a few steps I am across from Mercy, pulling out a chair from the table and sitting with her. I want to reach out and take her hands, to stop them from shaking, but I don't.

"We don't know how it happened exactly or why."

Mercy lowers her head. A single tear trickles down her face and splashes against the table. "Is that what I did to Lyla?"

Chapter Eighteen

Mercy

I want to die. For the first time since all of this happened, I honestly wish that I was dead. Death has to be better than this. What I just saw, what Nathaniel did, that can't be me. Without any memory of what happened after I passed out in the alley, I'll never know exactly how I got into Lyla's body, but if it looks anything like what Nathaniel had done, I'll never be able to forgive myself.

Repeating my question, I ask again, "Did I do that to her, Gage?"

"No. No!"

Gage looks pained. Whether he's lying or not, I want to believe him.

"I was there with you, remember?" He reaches out, takes my hands, and pulls me closer to him across the table. "Look at me, Mercy."

Lifting my head to meet his gaze, I see the sincerity, the

kindness in his eyes. Not deserving such a look, I turn away and rest my forehead on my arm.

Gage squeezes my hands. His grip is intense, a bit too forceful, but it's exactly what I need. I need someone to hold me together because I know at any moment I'm going to fall apart.

"Gage, do you want me to keep going?"

I'd forgotten Zee was in the room until he spoke. For a huge man he has an uncanny ability to remain still and quiet.

Gage nods to Zee and the screen changes again. He angles himself toward me and says, "I'm sorry. There's no easy way to do this."

Sitting up straight, I pulled away from him as a familiar image appears before me. My mouth falls open as all the air pushes from my lungs.

I'm looking at my mother.

Her arms are bound behind her back. Her once beautiful auburn hair is matted to her head like it hasn't been washed or combed in days. Her white gown is dirty, torn at the hem.

She's in the same courtroom I'd seen earlier. She faces the same panel of judges, each one wearing the same scowl they'd worn when facing Nathaniel.

"You are a traitor, Ariana. Save yourself and confess," says a man who could easily be one hundred and ten years old.

"No!" she cries out.

The chair hits the floor when I stand. Mesmerized I walk to the screen, wanting so badly to reach out and touch her. My mother.

A frail, female council member points a finger at Ariana. "This is your last chance. Confess, or suffer the same fate as Nathaniel."

My mother's expression changes from one of pain to one of defiance. It throws me off kilter as her eyes narrow, burning yellow fire. "You can't stop me. No one can."

"We'll see about that." The old man signals to someone off screen.

The doors at the back of the courtroom open and four soldiers march in, Gage at the lead, followed by Zee, Jinx, and Rae.

Ariana lowers her head, peering out at the four who stand before her. Despite being confined, she looks ready to fight. A snarl forms at her lips. I back away, not recognizing this part of her. This is not the mother I knew.

"You've raised an army," Arianna hisses. "You wage war against us."

The head councilman speaks. "It is you who wage war! We will simply put an end to it."

"Fools," Arianna roars.

The floor of the courtroom rocks slowly. A rumble shakes the pews. Ariana lets out an inhuman roar as the ties that bind her split apart. Just as I'd watch Nathaniel minutes before, my mother's body shatters like glass, shards flying in all directions.

"No!" I scream.

"Finish this," the head council member directs Gage and the others. They disappear in pursuit of Ariana.

My chest constricts. I can feel the fury gaining momentum as my breathing becomes rapid and shallow. Heat like I've never felt before courses through my veins. The disturbing images I'd just witnessed fuel my rage.

Learning I am a Breacher is nothing compared to this. My mother is not only a Breacher, she's evil. Pure evil. All the memories I have of her, all the sweetness, the kisses goodnight, the way she hugged me when I cried; it's all lies, nothing but a cover for her true self.

The room around me starts to sway.

"Mercy?" Gage's voice sounds distant, like he's calling to me from far away. "Mercy! Can you hear me?"

Part of me wants to answer him, but the other part wants to succumb. The heat that courses through me is both intoxicating and numbing. It drags me down, pulls at the edges.

"She's going to jump!" I hear Zee yell.

There's movement around me, yanking and pulling me, sometimes hurting me, but it's beyond my grasp. What is right within my reach is the warmth and so I settle into it, like dipping myself into a hot bath. I call to it to wash over me.

Suddenly, I feel the most intense, most searing pain of my entire life. It's as though the flesh is being pulled from my bones. Someone cries out; it's probably me, but I don't recognize the scream.

The pain worsens and, this time, when I hear myself cry out it scares me. The separation between mind and body is jarring. I can feel the pain, but at the same time it's like watching it happen to someone else.

Hands clamp down upon my shoulders, forcing me down. My wrists and ankles are bound. I thrash against the restraints, but it's no use. Immobilized, there's nothing to do but think of the pain. The pain.

Fighting, struggling, it's no use. I'm trapped within the agony.

And then it's gone. Just like that my body goes still.

I wake sometime later to the glare of harsh white lights. I squeeze my eyes shut and turn my head. Still restrained, I'm not able to move around much.

"She's waking up," I hear Rae speak from somewhere to my left.

"Give me a minute with her," Gage says.

"I'll be right outside," Rae tells him.

Their words move like smoke around my head.

"I'll be fine," Gage says.

I hear Rae's heels clack against the floor, growing softer as she moves farther away. A door, heavy from the sound of it, opens and closes.

Blinking against the light, I try again to open my eyes. The light is less harsh, blocked by Gage who is leaning over me.

"I'm going to loosen the straps, okay?"

Within seconds the tension around my ankles and wrists dissipates.

"Let me help you sit up." Gage slips his hand under my shoulders. "Take it easy."

He lifts me into a sitting position. My head throbs. My wrists and ankles are raw and covered in bruises and burns from the restraints.

"Drink this." Gage tips a paper cup to my lips. A cool liquid washes over my parched gums and throat.

"Thank you," I croak. Taking the cup from him I swallow two more generous helpings.

Gage nods in approval. When I finish drinking he takes the cup from me and sets it on the counter. The room is like an examination room at a doctor's office: crisp, white, and sterile. There are a couple of cabinets, a sink, and a biohazard waste box.

"How are you feeling?" he asks me.

"Like I've been hit by a truck," I answer. "What happened?"

"You tried to jump from Lyla's body," he says with a tinge

of anger to his voice.

The straightforwardness of his answer throws me off a bit. Apparently he's finished sugarcoating things for me.

"That's not possible." I wouldn't do that to Lyla. I know that if I leave her body I'll kill her.

"Luckily, we were able to stop you."

"But this doesn't make sense. You said that the only way for me to leave Lyla's body was if she died."

Gage turns his back to me. He grips the edges of the counter. The muscles of his shoulders and back strain the fabric of the dark, gray shirt he wears.

A sickening thought occurs to me. "Did I try and kill her? I mean did I do something harmful to myself. To harm Lyla?"

"No," he answers, not turning around.

Regaining my strength, I hop off the table I'd been strapped to and step closer to him. "Then how? I don't get it."

"I know why Nathaniel is after you," Gage whispers.

His words do nothing to alleviate my fears or calm my nerves. My patience is thinning.

"So then tell me."

Gage paces back and forth, wearing tracks into the white floor. When he stops he put his hands on his hips and faces me square on. "There's only been one other case of a Breacher being able to jump from one body to another without killing its host first."

I know exactly where he's headed and he looks like he's having trouble saying the words, so I help him out. "My mother."

Most girls hope to inherit traits from their mothers, like shiny hair, or eye color. Some are lucky enough to have life skills passed on to them like cooking or sewing or snaking a drain—my mother could do all of that. She was also spontaneous and generous and had a wicked sense of humor. Any of those things she could've bestowed upon me, and yet I get stuck with body stealing … and God knows what else.

He nods. "She was extremely powerful."

"I'm starting to understand that."

Something dawns on me. A tiny glimmer of hope begins to burn inside of me.

"Wait a minute. If I can leave Lyla's body without killing it, then I can get out of it right now without hurting her."

"Mercy, it's not that simple." Gage tries to reason with me, but I'm not hearing any of it.

"It is! It is that simple. I can make this right."

"Mercy." Gage takes me by the shoulders. "Lyla's dead."

No. I don't believe him.

"How do you know she's dead?"

"Experience, mostly," he answers matter-of-factly. "In all my years as a Hunter I've never seen it any other way. Breachers take over bodies and there's nothing left of the original person."

I sink into the bed again. Defeat and grief twist around me and squeeze. It's difficult for me to breathe.

Gage kneels on the floor in front of me. "I'm sorry that all of this is happening, Mercy." He covers my hands in his. "I wish there was more that I could do, to somehow make this easier for you."

Such tenderness in his voice and in his expression, I've never really seen this side of him before. I know he cares about me, or something like that, but these words are different. He wants to take my pain away and he feels guilty that he can't. He feels powerless. For the first time I see his vulnerability.

Overcome by everything, my eyes pool with tears. Though I want to hold them in, a few break loose and slither down my cheeks. With his hand cupping the side of my face, Gage brushes away the tears with his thumb.

Before I know it, I'm in *that* moment, the one that happens right before two people kiss. He leans toward me and I reciprocate. His breath lingers on my lips.

The door slams open and Rae bursts in. Gage and I jump apart.

Rae groans. "Oh, you've got to be kidding me."

Gage stands, pulling away from me. "Leave it alone, Rae."

There's no chance of that. Rae glares at me then rolls her eyes in disgust.

"You're ruining him," she says sharply. "I hope you know that. The Gage I know would never act like this. He was our leader, the one who kept all of us in check whenever humanity crept in." She says humanity like it's a dirty word.

"Rae, stop," Gage says.

Rae spins around to face Gage, a look of disgust on her face. "I don't even know who you are anymore," she seethes. She turns again, giving me one more glare full of hatred, and then she leaves.

"She's pleasant," I quip.

"She's right," Gage replies coldly.

His words sting. I stare at him in shock. Gone is the Gage from just a few seconds before. The tenderness, the vulnerability, is gone. In its place is Gage, the soldier. A tremble of fear rips through me like icicles down my spine.

"Let's go," he says sternly and leaves the room.

Chapter Nineteen

Gage

I keep my distance from Mercy as we walk down the hall, Rae's words repeating in my head. Hers was the reminder I needed to jolt me back to the present, to keep me focused on my job. As a Hunter, I'm sworn to track and kill Breachers, to not fall in love with them.

Fall in love. Is that what I'm doing? Not being familiar with the feelings associated with love, I'm not quite sure. I've seen what love does to humans. It makes them weak, it muddies their judgment; it makes them do things they normally wouldn't. *Sounds about right.*

And it certainly does explain my behavior in all of this. Why do I care so deeply about what happens to her? Why can't I just do my job? I've been saying that it is because of Nathaniel, that I have to know what he's up to, but is that all, or is there something more?

Without asking, I borrow Rae's car and drive Mercy home.

We don't speak, which only adds to the tension, but what can I possibly say to her? Apologizing for almost kissing her doesn't seem right, but ignoring her isn't right either.

My less than stellar driving isn't helping matters. Every time I take a sharp turn or skid to a stop, Mercy stares deeper and deeper out the window. Her avoidance is killing me. It would've been better if she said something, or yelled at me for acting like an idiot.

Since she didn't, it left me wondering if she thought our almost kiss was a mistake. It bothers me more than I'm comfortable with, thinking that she might feel relieved that Rae came in and broke things up.

I have to get my mind right. These thoughts aren't good for me, especially now.

Things keep getting more and more complicated. Mercy's attempt at jumping from Lyla's body only strengthens my belief that she's no ordinary Breacher. If she can jump from body to body without killing the host, then we're in real trouble.

I had no choice but to lie to her, to tell her that Lyla is dead. It was the only way to keep her from leaving Lyla's body.

So far I've been able to keep The Assembled at bay. They trust me to take care of things, to use Mercy as bait to draw Nathaniel out and kill him. Though I plan to try and reason with them after, to try and convince them to let me put Mercy back in her body and to live out her normal life, I know that chance is gone if they find out her true power.

The thought occurs to me then that Nathaniel has known all along what she can do. After all, it wouldn't be that big of a stretch for Mercy to have inherited the full scope of her mother's powers. I'm an idiot for not considering the possibility.

I thought I could give her a chance by attempting to return

her to her body, but now I'm not sure that's such a good idea. It's not like I can let her go through life jumping from body to body at whim. The power is too intoxicating. She'd be able to manipulate anyone she wants. There's no way The Assembled would allow it. They'd insist that she be destroyed.

What kills me the most is that part of me knows they'd be right. It doesn't matter that Mercy has no interest in breaching, that she isn't controlled by her impulses. No creature should have that much power. Free will cannot be tampered with. What if she sees it as harmless to breach the store clerk so that she doesn't have to pay, or breach a teacher to get good grades? Those things might seem harmless, inconsequential to her, but to The Assembled those are crimes punishable by death. And it doesn't matter if she promises never to breach. The Assembled will never trust her, never believe her.

I pull the car to a stop in front of Lyla's house. The early morning light of dawn is just beginning to peek over the house.

"It wasn't my intention to keep you all night," I tell her. My tone is too formal. I can tell from the look on her face she feels the same way. She's noticed the shift in me, the change, and in return, she's pulling away. I don't like it.

"It's fine," she says tersely.

She gets out of the car and slams the door.

Chapter Twenty

Mercy

I expect Kate to be asleep. What I don't expect is Jay asleep in Lyla's bed. He looks so sweet and peaceful curled around Lyla's pillow. I hate to wake him.

Nudging him lightly, I whisper, "Jay." He grunts and rolls over to face the wall. I shake his shoulder. "Jay, wake up."

He rubs his hands over his face. "What time is it?"

"Around four thirty."

"Are you just getting in?"

"Yeah. Did Kate notice I was gone?"

"I covered for you."

"Thanks."

"You want to tell me what happened?"

I did, but exhaustion is wearing me down. "I will, but right now I need sleep."

Jay pulls back the covers and makes space for me.

"Are you sure this is okay?"

"Mercy, it's fine. Just get in."

Slipping out of my Keds, I slide in next to him still fully clothed. Jay's warm body is exactly what I need to feel safe. The steady rhythm of his breathing is like a lullaby.

But just as I'm about to fall asleep the strangest thing happens. I'm no longer in the bed, but rather I'm standing across the room watching, like a fly on the wall.

Lyla and Jay are stretched out on her bed studying. Jay's head is propped up on several pillows. Playfully, Lyla runs her toe along his leg.

"Ly, I'm trying to study," Jay teasingly scolds.

"I *am* studying."

"You're trying to distract me." Jay sets his book down on his chest.

Lyla coyly smiles. "No I'm not."

"I have to do well on this test tomorrow," Jay insists.

"Fine." Lyla retracts her leg. "But I invoke the one finger rule."

"And what is that?"

"Just one finger." She stretches her hand until it meets Jay's wrist. "Touching at all times."

His left eyebrow arches, questioning her motives. She bats her eyelashes until Jay has no choice but to give into her.

"One finger." Jay's index finger pokes the soft skin on the inside of Lyla's elbow.

Jay's one finger can't remain still and soon begins exploring. Before long all ten fingers on both hands are searching, seeking her out. Lyla angles her hips toward Jay and with one swift motion he hoists her up so that she's straddling him. His hands explore under her shirt. She leans forward until her mouth is right above his.

I bolt up straight. Jay is still next to me in bed sleeping soundly. It must've been a dream. I fall back against the pillow and immediately drift off.

Sometime later I wake to sunlight streaming through the windows. The clock next to Lyla's bed reads two thirty PM. Jay is gone and I've slept the day away. I could easily bury my head under the pillow and kept right on sleeping, but I know I have to get up.

After I shower and change clothes I begin the hunt for food. Traditionally, Lyla's house resembles Mother Hubbard's cupboard. I manage to scrounge up a bowl of cereal and drink the very last of the orange juice.

The newspaper is on the table. I flip it open and read all about Mr. Andreas's apparent suicide. He lived alone, had no family to speak of, and even though they scrounged up a few teachers and students to say some nice things about him, it was clear that Mr. Andreas had been something of a loner, which is probably why it was so easy for Nathaniel to take over his body.

Sometimes I still can't believe that I'm in Lyla's body. I realize now that it no longer feels like carrying around a flesh suit, as Nathaniel called it. Without even noticing, I've begun to adapt to her height, her gait, even the way she slurps milk from the spoon. With each passing hour I lose more and more of myself and become her.

It makes me wonder if I will lose myself entirely. Will I let go of who I am and become her? I hope not. Before my thoughts can wander even farther, the phone rings.

"Hello," I say as I pick up the receiver.

"Lyla, it's Mr. Clare."

Dad! My heart sinks to my feet. A lump rises in my throat

and my jaw tightens as I fight the tears.

"Lyla, are you still there?"

"Yes, I'm here."

"Something's happened. I don't want to frighten you, but I need you and Kate to come over as soon as possible."

I assure him that I'll be right there. Then I call over to Wally's, but I get the answering machine. I leave a hasty message and then try Kate on her cell. Again, there's no answer and I leave a message.

After I hang up, I run out the front door and straight to Jay's house. Luckily, I have Lyla's athletic body to carry me and it doesn't take me long. I hope that Kate will get my messages and that she'll be only a few minutes behind me. Whatever my dad wants to tell me, I don't want to hear it alone.

When I reach Jay's front door I hesitate, but only for a second. As myself, I would've knocked. I would've waited for someone to answer the door. But I know this is not how Lyla would do it, and I am more than glad to be able to walk right in.

"Jay!" I call as I run toward his room. "Jay!"

It doesn't appear that anyone is home. I search and search, but I find no one. That is, until I get to Jay's mom's bedroom.

Her feet are the first thing I spot poking out on the far side of the bed. I slow my steps and inch closer.

"Mrs. Sheller?"

There's no answer. As I creep closer, I know something is terribly wrong. She lies face down in a pool of blood.

"Oh, my God!"

I rush to her side, but am careful not to touch her. I don't know what to do. "Mrs. Sheller, please wake up!" I plead.

Blood trickles from the corner of her mouth. I scramble to

my feet and reach into my back pocket for my cell phone, but it isn't there. *Shit!* I run to the kitchen and try to dial nine-one-one. There's no tone. *Shit!*

I sprint next door to my house. I don't bother knocking there either. My dad is startled when I come crashing through the door.

I blurt out, "Next door! Mrs. Sheller! Not moving! Lots of blood!"

His eyes go wide.

"Call nine-one-one!" I bark at him.

He half stumbles, half runs for the phone and gives the nine-one-one Operator the information, or pieces of information, rather, that I'd given him.

My hands tremble while we wait. The Operator keeps my dad on the phone until the sound of the ambulance fills the streets.

We both rush outside to greet the Emergency Service Technicians. I explain how I found her. They won't let me or my father inside the house again. Instead, we're forced to wait outside.

After a few tense minutes my dad puts his hand on my shoulder and asks, "Did you call Jay?"

Jay! Oh, my God! What the hell was I thinking?

My dad, always intuitive, reads my expression and says calmly, "It's okay. We'll call him together."

We walk back to my house and place the call. Jay, like Kate, doesn't answer. I don't know what to say to his voicemail, so I just tell him to call me immediately.

As we make our way back outside, the EMTs come rushing out of Jay's house. Mrs. Sheller's body is still. There are bandages around her head and an IV sticking out of her arm.

"Is she going to be okay?" my father asks.

"We're trying to get her stable. Taking her to Sutter General."

"Can we come with you?" It's what Lyla would've insisted.

"No room. We'll meet you there."

The EMTs load Jay's mom into the ambulance and back out of the driveway. The taillights fade as the ambulance speeds off toward the hospital.

"I'll drive," my dad tells me as he ushers me to the car.

Chapter Twenty-One

The ride to the hospital is torture and not just because my dad is an overly cautious driver. The smell of his aftershave fills the car. The way his hands grip the wheel at the precise ten and two positions, the way he always signals before turning, it's all so *him*. And it makes my insides burn not to be able to talk to him like I normally would.

The radio is turned to his favorite Pandora station. My dad's inner hippie is evident by his musical selection of sixties and seventies acid rock. In most aspects my dad plays the part of the college professor to a T. He has the tweed jacket with the leather elbow patches, the ratty old briefcase that he refuses to replace. But that's his professional life. I know him better.

We find a place to park in the same lot where I confessed the truth to Jay. This is the second time in two days that some tragedy has drawn my father to this hospital. It's not been a good week for any of us.

The emergency room is bustling. The noise, the rushing

around, it's all too chaotic. My dad ushers me over to the same waiting room chairs where it all began. It's surreal and nauseating.

We sit for a while and nothing happens. No one comes to talk to us. Neither Jay nor Kate arrive.

Lyla would not sit still. She would not wait any longer. She would charge up to the nurse's station and demand to know what was happening. But before I can do that, I have to find out why my dad called me over to his house in the first place.

I turn to him and say, "You called earlier and said that something had happened. What did you want to tell me?"

"I don't know if now is the right time, but then again, there may never be a right time to tell you."

My father has a tendency to do this, to consider things out loud as opposed to in his head. I nearly smile, but I'm too impatient.

"Just tell me, please."

"Okay." He clears his throat. "It seems as though the hospital, well, the morgue, has misplaced Mercy's body."

Holy shit! My body is missing? Every time I think things can't get any worse, they do.

"What are we going to do?"

"The morgue assures me it's a clerical error of some kind and that everything will be fine."

"Do you believe them?"

"I have to."

Every inch of me is tingling and burning, churning with anger, fear, and agitation. It's impossible for me to sit still any longer.

"I can't take this! I'm going to find out what's going on with Mrs. Sheller."

My dad does not look surprised by my outburst. He's seen

Lyla in action before, which is why he doesn't stop me from storming off. What I really want to do is find my body, but I don't even know where to start. I have to focus on the task at hand.

Four women man the nurse's station. "Hey!" I slap my hand on the counter. "Can one of you give me some information about Mrs. Sheller?"

Each nurse wears an expression of varying shades of annoyance. Only one looks moderately concerned. The rest look overworked and not in the mood to deal with an unruly teenager.

The most senior looking nurse slides a pen into her breast pocket and asks me, "Are you family, hon?"

"Well, I'm dating her son. So kinda."

"I'm sorry we can't give information out unless your immediate family."

I am not going to give up. Lyla would not have given up. "Look, she's divorced. Her ex lives in Utah. I tried calling her son, but he didn't answer. So I'm it for right now. I'm her family."

The nurse comes closer to the glass partition. "Have a seat, hon." She dismisses me.

Grudgingly, I walk heavy-footed back to the chairs. When I get there, my dad is on his phone.

"I left another message for Jay," he tells me. "And one for Kate. I'm surprised they're not here yet."

"Me too," I answer.

An unsettling feeling, a new kind of fear grows inside me. It isn't right that both Jay and Kate aren't here. And if I add in what happened to Mrs. Sheller, there's no escaping the possibility that something much worse happened. I just don't know what it is. Yet.

Chapter Twenty-Two

Gage

I can't sleep. I'm stressed, I'm exhausted and my eyes refuse to close. My brain refuses to rest. I'm tired of wearing out the floors in the warehouse. I need to get out. The streets are quiet. Walking will clear my head.

Resigned to my duties, I know what I have to do. No longer can I let my feelings for Mercy get in the way of my work. Rae, Zee, and Jinx trust me as their leader. They've been willing to go against the orders of The Assembled because I've asked them to, but I know now that I was wrong in asking.

I am wrong on all fronts. It doesn't matter why Nathaniel wants Mercy. My job is not to ask questions, not to reason with Breacher mentality. It's time to stop trying to understand Nathaniel, to figure out why he is the way he is. In the end, does it really matter anyway? Nathaniel is a criminal. Period. I was selected to kill him and at every turn I've hesitated. No more. My only job is to destroy Breachers. And that's exactly what I intend to do. I have to destroy Mercy.

In order to rectify the mess I've made, my first order of business is to collect Mercy. I can't let her run around in Lyla's body anymore. I shouldn't have allowed it to go on this long.

Changing direction, I decide not to return to the warehouse, but instead to go directly to Lyla's house and find Mercy. I will bring in her in, hand her over to Rae, and let Rae do what she does best: extract a Breacher from a body.

When Mercy is out of Lyla's body, I'll alert a Guide to help her cross over. It's the one exception I'm willing to make. Most Breachers are jailed, sentenced to an eternity in purgatory, but this is not a fate I want for Mercy. She's an unknowing Breacher. And it's partly my fault she even left her body. I should've stopped her way before the night of her birthday party.

With Mercy out of the way, I'll be clear to hunt and kill Nathaniel and finally finish out my term of service.

I decide all of this by the time I reach Lyla's house. It doesn't take me long to figure out that Mercy isn't there and that she left in a hurry. The doors are unlocked and her cell phone is on the kitchen table.

My senses kick into high gear as I run from Lyla's to Mercy's. Getting there does nothing to alleviate my suspicions. Mercy's house is also empty and in a state of disarray. A book is knocked to the floor, the spine cracking under the weight of the pages. From everything I know of Mercy's father, he would never discard a book in such a way.

Leaving Mercy's house, I see that there is something eerie about Jay's house as well. The front door is wide open, yet no lights are on in the front rooms. Small tire tracks in the carpet lead me to the rear bedroom where I find a dried ring of blood.

It will take me too long to run to the hospital. Hotwiring whatever car I find in the garage seems like a much better plan. The garage door clatters open to reveal a late model Honda Odyssey. *You've got to be kidding me,* I groan. Of all the cars in the world, I find a mommy mobile.

Turns out, minivans have more horsepower than I imagined. In no time I'm at the hospital and running through the emergency room doors. There's no sign of Mercy anywhere.

I find her father sitting alone in the waiting room area, but I don't make myself known to him. Instead I attempt to find Mercy.

A quick check of the nearest bathrooms and vending machine areas and there's still no sign of her. Worry pushes me to keep looking. Creeping past the nurse's station, I steal a quick look at their assignment board and determine that it's Jay's mother who has been injured. I locate her room, hoping that I'll find Mercy.

When I don't find her in the room, the worry that I've been feeling morphs into panic.

Out in the hall, I look right and left, hoping, waiting for a sign. A scream rings out in the stairwell and I set off running.

With my full weight behind me, I shove open the door and take the stairs two at a time until I reach the roof.

Nathaniel has Mercy. He's dragging her across the graveled roof. Tiny pieces of rock kick up against her feet as she struggles to pull away from him.

"Let her go!" I yell.

Nathaniel smiles at me. His grip tightens around Mercy's arms.

"Back away, Nathaniel, or I swear I'll kill you right here."

"Promises, promises, little brother."

Mercy's head whips around toward me. She looks from me to him and back to me. The look on her face tells me she doesn't know which one of us she hates more.

"You and your secrets, Gage." Nathaniel clucks his tongue, admonishing me in a haughty tone. Then he focuses his attention on Mercy. "I told you the Hunters lie, Mercy."

"I didn't lie," I fire.

"Omission is the same thing. Or didn't they teach you that at Hunter school?"

"You're brothers?" Mercy squirms away from Nathaniel and he lets her. He's enjoying this.

"What are you doing here, Nathaniel?" I ask, keeping my focus.

"Same thing you are; checking on our girl."

I don't like his tone. The smugness of it makes my skin crawl.

"There were Breachers lurking about. I chased them off." He leans into Mercy's neck and whispers at her throat, "You can thank me later." Mercy shivers.

"I should kill you right now," I spit at him.

He laughs. "You keep saying that, and yet here I am."

Mercy's expression is one of stone. She speaks through clenched teeth, "Explain to me exactly what is going on. NO more lies."

Nathaniel faces her directly so that I can no longer see her face. "If you're looking for the truth, I'd direct your questions to me."

"Mercy, don't!" I attempt to get at her, but she holds her hand up to stop me.

With pure venom in her voice she says to me, "You had your chance."

Nathaniel glances over his shoulder at me and flashes a toothy grin. The pleasure he's getting out of all of this makes me violently angry. He isn't concerned about Mercy's feelings or how she'll react to what he's about to tell her. He only wants to see me suffer.

Nathaniel strides slowly to the other side of Mercy. He stands behind her and puts his arm around her shoulder. She tenses, but does not move away.

"See, Gage here," Nathaniel starts, "was actually made from me. Like a rib from Adam, he is made of me. We are one. The Assembled, in their infinite wisdom, thought that someone who was part of me would have a better chance of killing me. He is made of me just like you were made of your mother."

Mercy's whole body is rigid. I want to put an end to it, but I can't risk it in this uncontrolled setting. Without backup, without the restraints, it's very likely that Mercy will jump. I have to remain calm so that she remains calm.

Mercy directs a question at me. "If you were made to kill Nathaniel, was I made to kill my mother?"

Yes. The answer is yes. The Assembled thought Ariana should suffer the ultimate consequence and be taken down by the one person she loved unconditionally. It was a piece of information I'd never planned on telling Mercy because there was no point.

"You were, my dear. But don't worry. Gage took care of that messy work for you."

Mercy's legs liquidate. Nathanial catches her before she hits the ground.

"Easy," Nathaniel says. "I've gotcha."

"Don't touch me!" Mercy shoves away from him. I take two tiny steps toward her. "You!" Mercy shouts at me. "Stay the hell away from me!"

"Uh-oh. I think we're going to lose her," Nathaniel's tone borders on glee.

I rush to her side, grab her by the arms and shake her, but I know that she's losing her battle. She crumples to the ground.

"Mercy!" I yell in desperation, dropping to my knees. "Don't! You have to control it. You can stop it. You have to try."

"Gage," Nathaniel scolds. "You never learn. Step aside."

Nathaniel shoves me aside and scoops Mercy up into his arms. He holds her face in his hands and smashes his lips to hers in one swift motion.

He gently pulls back and says to me, "That, little brother, is what humans and Breachers alike respond to. Desire." Nathaniel wipes his mouth.

"What did you do?" I charge at Nathaniel.

"Exactly what you couldn't do. I stopped her from breaching," Nathaniel responds. Mercy breaks away from Nathaniel.

I rear back and slug Nathaniel right across the chin. Unfazed, Nathaniel rubs his jaw and laughs. I am ready to hit him again, but Mercy jumps between us.

"Stop! Just stop! This is insane."

"Mercy, I can explain everything," I start.

She cuts me off. "There is nothing you can say to make this any better. Nothing. So don't bother."

"Why don't you just tell her the truth, Gage? Hasn't this song and dance gone on long enough?" Nathaniel chimes in.

"You," I point at Nathaniel, "need to shut the hell up."

"Someone tell me what the hell is going on. Stop talking in code and tell me the truth."

"Truth? That's not really a Hunter priority," Nathaniel says with a mocking tone. "It's more about versions of the truth, right, brother?"

"Fine. Then you tell me," Mercy says to Nathaniel.

Nathaniel's eyes dance with delight. "I'd be more than happy to explain to you Gage's plan—how he will use you as bait to draw me out and kill us both. But we have more pressing matters at hand. Like how someone kidnapped a couple of humans you're fond of."

Mercy narrows her eyes at him. "What are you talking about?"

"What do you know?" I ask Nathaniel.

Nathaniel scrunches his face and shrugs his shoulders pretending to be innocent.

"Stop messing around, Nathaniel. We're wasting time," I say. Irritation and impatience echo each word.

"Let's just say I'm no longer your biggest problem," Nathaniel speaks in a cool tone.

"What's that supposed to mean?" I ask him.

"It means, dear brother," Nathaniel leans in close to Mercy and whispers against her neck, "that Mommy isn't as dead as we thought."

Chapter Twenty-Three

My cell phone buzzes inside my jacket. I check the caller ID. Rae's name flashes on the screen.

I don't get to say hello. As soon as I pick up she barks, "Something's going on, Gage! The alarms are sounding!"

In the background I can hear the wail of the siren. "Where are Zee and Jinx?" I ask.

Rae's heels pound against the floor as she runs. "They went to check the perimeter!" she yells.

"I'm on my way."

I'm about to hang up the phone when I hear Rae curse. "What?" I ask her. "What's wrong?"

"The body is gone! Someone took the body!"

She screams, and then the line goes dead.

"Shit!" I yell. "This can't be happening!"

"Trouble, little brother?"

The entire situation has gotten out of hand. It isn't supposed to be like this. The plan was to return Mercy to her body, to set everything right. For the first time I feel completely out of control, helpless.

"Gage, what's going on?" Mercy's face is etched with concern.

"We have to move," I tell them. "Now."

Sprinting for the stairwell, I don't look back to see if they're following me. I know they will be. Part of the demented connection between Nathaniel and me is that we sense each other's emotions. We feel each other's pain and joy. Which is why when he kissed Mercy I felt …

There's no time for that now! I push the thought from my head and focus on Rae, Jinx, Zee, and whatever danger awaits us at the warehouse.

Mercy climbs into the backseat of the car, Nathaniel rides shotgun and I drive like mad. We make it back in record time, violating every traffic law imaginable.

Mercy is the last to exit the car. She slams the door. "Jesus Christ! Are you trying to kill us?"

"What?"

"You tailgate! You nearly killed that old lady back there when you blew through that stop sign! You are the worst driver ever!"

"I am not."

"Oh, really? Did you notice that you're parked on the curb?"

Nathaniel steps between us. "We'll let you drive next time," he says to Mercy. "But right now we have bigger problems."

The warehouse is on fire. Black smoke fills the sky as balls of flame blow out windows, shattered glass scattering the sidewalks.

The three of us stand and gawk. Nathaniel's trepidation, his momentary pause makes me even more nervous. Neither one of us know what we're up against. But whatever it is, we're on the same side against it, of that I'm sure.

"Stay here," I say to Mercy.

"We can't leave her out here alone," Nathaniel says.

"My team is in there. I can't protect them and her at the same time. You stay with her."

"Gage, you can't go in there alone. You'll get yourself killed." Mercy's voice is anything but calm.

That right there is the reason I know Mercy is different from all the other Breachers I've encountered. Even after everything I've put her through, she's still concerned for my safety.

"Nathaniel, I'm asking you to make sure nothing happens to her."

"I won't let her out of my sight," Nathaniel assures me.

Mercy looks like she wants to protest, but I don't give her a chance. I take off running. When I reach the outer door I can see that a bomb started the fire. The entire security system is a heaping pile of melted wire.

Using my shoulder I shove the inner door open. Intense heat and thick smoke blur my vision. A shower of rain falls from the sprinkler system, drenching me instantly. My jacket is no substitute for an oxygen mask, but it's all I have. I throw it over my face to shield myself.

Once I hit the interior of the warehouse, the smoke clears a bit and I'm able to see. I run for the Observation Deck.

Jinx's body slumps against the controls. His shirt, soaked through with blood, reveals three sizable holes in his chest. I pull him upright, hoping to see some sign of life in him, but he's gone.

There's no time to mourn. No time for sorrow. These are human emotions that I can't afford to succumb to, not while I have work to do.

"Zee! Rae!" I yell as I continue my search.

The library is empty and shows evidence of a struggle. Tables and chairs are toppled, the large screen riddled with holes. Zee would never go down without a fight.

Rae is right. Mercy's body is gone. But nothing else seems to be missing. The body is what they came for.

I circle back through the halls and out to the garage. That's where I find Zee sprawled across the floor. His body, too, is full of holes with spurts of blood dripping and oozing onto the concrete.

Kneeling next to him, I feel for a pulse, but there isn't one. Zee is dead.

Dripping wet and ready to kill whoever I cross, I push on, searching for Rae and hoping against hope that I will find her alive.

It's entirely my fault that all of this happened, that Jinx and Zee are dead. All of it is my fault. I will never be able to forgive myself for not doing my job. My feelings for Mercy and my curiosity about Nathaniel's plan distracted me. I brought this upon my team. If I'd done my work like I was supposed to, if I'd destroyed Mercy when I had the chance, they'd still be alive.

I had my chance to kill Mercy the night I killed her mother, Ariana. Mercy was just a child. She wouldn't have seen me coming, wouldn't have been able to breach before I put an end to her.

If I had done it then, maybe none of this would've happened. Logically, I know this is a possibility.

This is no longer about Nathaniel. He didn't do this; he isn't the one who kidnapped Jay and Kate. Nathaniel isn't the one that set fire to this building. He didn't killed Jinx or Zee.

There's only one person I can think of that could manage to pull this off, who could create this much chaos in such a short amount of time. And if what I think is true, then we are in more trouble than any of us imagined.

Chapter Twenty-Four

Mercy

Waiting on the sidewalk is not the answer. I know it and I can tell Nathaniel knows it by the way he's pacing and fidgeting. We should never have let Gage go charging into the building alone. For all we know he could be dead by now and we're just standing around like idiots.

"Don't even think about it," Nathaniel says, shaking his head at me. "It's much too dangerous."

"It's dangerous for Gage," I remind him. "Not that you would care."

He flashes me a look. I've struck a nerve. "You do care, don't you?"

Turning his back to me, Nathaniel continues to pace.

"You care. And it's killing you to stand here and do nothing! So let's go. Gage needs our help."

Nathaniel considers for a moment and then forcefully he grasps my hand and leads me into the building.

Though the smoke isn't thick, it lingers in the air, shrouding our visibility.

"Stay close to me," Nathaniel instructs. "And if I say run, run. Got it?"

I nod and huddle as close to him as I can without actually touching him. After the whole kiss experience, I can't be this near to him without being painfully aware of the energy that courses between us.

We find Jinx at the Observation Deck. Without thinking I bury my head into Nathaniel's shoulder, unable to look at the body. Nathaniel hurries us along through the building.

He pulls up short in a room that looks very much like a hospital room. I've never seen it before, but I have the strangest sense of déjà vu.

Stepping away from Nathaniel, I stand in the center of the room.

He eyes me skeptically and asks, "What is it?"

"I don't know," I reply. "It's the strangest feeling." I turn in small circles, waiting for the answer to pop into my head as to why I should feel such a connection to a place I've never been, but nothing comes to mind.

"Do you know what this room is for?" I ask Nathaniel.

He looks around and answers, "I have a guess."

"Care to clue me in?"

"No." Gage's appearance in the entryway startles me. "He doesn't."

"We found Jinx," I tell him.

"Zee's dead too," Gage adds.

"I'm sorry." My voice is small.

Awkward silence prevails. Nathaniel and Gage eye each other, exchanging looks and unspoken words. All of us need a minute to wrap our heads around the events that have transpired. In just a short time, Jay and Kate were kidnapped, Jay's mom was attacked, and Jinx and Zee were killed.

"What do we do now?" My voice breaks the silence.

"I'm thinking," Gage answers.

"Wait!" A thought occurs to me. "Did you find Rae? Is she okay? Is she here?"

Gage slowly shakes his head. I don't know whether or not that means she's dead or alive.

"They took her." Nathaniel speaks in a cool tone. "Interesting."

"Why do you say it like that?" I ask.

Nathaniel tilts his head to the side and smirks at Gage. "Why don't we let him tell you."

"Not again." I turn to Gage. "Are you keeping more secrets from me?"

Gage's lips curl inward as he glowers at Nathaniel.

"Gage," I say again. "What's going on?"

His mouth barely moves when he says, "It's complicated."

Nathaniel laughs to himself. "That's an understatement."

I feel like the monkey in the middle. Their routine of knowing things that I don't know and keeping them from me is tiring. It's time to dig deep and find Lyla's strength.

Crossing my arms over my chest I pop one foot out, the way Lyla always does when she's being defiant or stubborn. "You two are going to tell me what's going on right now. Or I'm walking out this door and to hell with you both."

Nathaniel suppresses a smile while Gage's mouth hangs open.

"Well," I continue, "which is it gonna be?"

Gage blows out a big breath and begins, "They took Rae

because she possesses a unique set of skills."

"Yeah, so? I know there's more to it than that." I hold my ground, my strength and determination unwavering.

Gage, unable to meet my eyes, puts his hands on his hips and talks to the floor as he says, "Rae is our medic, our chemist. She's in charge of extractions."

Rae is the one who can pull a soul from a body. A shiver ripples up my spine.

"Was there a Breacher in this room?" Nathaniel asks, his face lit up with accusation. He's enjoying every second that Gage squirms.

"Yes," Gage answers tersely.

"And that's who they came for, am I right?" Nathaniel asks, though he clearly knows the answer.

"Yes," Gage says.

"I still don't get it. Who were you keeping here?" I ask.

Gage bites the inside of his lip, keeping his eyes glued to the floor.

"You've made quite the mess, haven't you, brother?" Nathaniel's tone is less gleeful and more rueful, as though for the first time he pities Gage.

I charge up to Gage and force him to look at me, to lock eyes with me before I ask again. "Who were you keeping here?"

"You."

This time I don't faint. The world doesn't fall out from under me. Instead, everything is very, very still.

Gage and I continue to stare at each other for several moments. I wait for him to blink or take it back or something, but instead he holds my glare.

After a few more beats I say, "You had my body here?"

Then I remember. "Fucking Christ! Is that why the morgue thinks they misplaced my body, because you took it?"

"Yes."

"But I thought I was dead."

His gaze reverts to the floor. "Not exactly."

"I think I need to sit down." My knees are locked into position and if I don't bend soon I might stay frozen forever.

Gage stole my body from the hospital. I'm not dead, so what does this mean? Am I in a coma? It doesn't make any sense. Why would he do such a thing? And why didn't he tell me?

It's Nathaniel who takes me by the elbow and lowers me in a nearby chair. With my head between my knees I hug my legs and try to keep steady.

Nathaniel says to me in a loving voice that I didn't know he was capable of, "I won't let anything happen to you."

I don't realize I'm crying until he wipes a tear from my cheek.

"Do you know where they might have taken her?" Gage directs his question at Nathaniel.

"I have a guess," Nathaniel replies.

The fact that my body had been here, in this damp and dark warehouse, right under my nose infuriates me to no end. But at the same time it gives me hope that maybe Nathaniel is wrong and that Gage wasn't planning on destroying me once he completed his mission. Maybe, just maybe, he meant to send me back, to my home, to my dad.

My dad! We left him at the hospital, alone. Anything could've happened to him by now and he will certainly be wondering what happened to me. Moreover, he'll be concerned when Jay and Kate never show up. I wonder if maybe I should try telling him the truth. But even if I convince him that I'm inside Lyla's body, I don't know how I can ever tell him about my mother.

My dad loves my mother wholeheartedly. To this day, when he mentions her, the edges of his mouth curl into a comfortable smile. He talks about her freely, often with tears, but also with laughter, telling me story after story. He doesn't want me to forget her and so he keeps her memory close.

How can I ever tell him who she really is?

With the meeting of the minds complete, Gage and Nathaniel return their attention to me.

"We should get out of here," Gage says. "It won't be long before the fire department arrives."

"Where are we going to go?" I ask.

"You are going to go home," Gage says to me. "It's safer for you there."

"It's safer for her with us," Nathaniel disagrees.

"I'm still not convinced of that," Gage argues.

"You can wait for the writing on the wall if you want, but that would be a waste of time. Face, it Gage," Nathaniel says, "Ariana is alive and well despite your best efforts. Not only is she here, but she's after Mercy and she's not going to stop until she gets what she wants."

And there it is, plain and simple, exactly what we're up against. My mother. Someday I'll force Gage to tell me the story of how he could've killed her and not killed her at the same time. But Nathaniel is right, we don't have time for stories right now.

We need a plan to get my friends back and to save Rae. And if my mother is even half of what I fear she might be, we're running out of time.

"I'm coming with you," I tell Gage. "I don't care if it's too dangerous and I don't care if it's not what you want. Jay and Kate are my friends and I'm going to help them and there's not a damn thing you can do about it." It's nearly word for word what Lyla would've said if she were here instead of me.

Gage doesn't put up a fight. The three of us set off. Our first priority is to check on my dad and Mrs. Sheller at the hospital. Her condition is improving and though it takes some serious lying on my part, I manage to convince my father that Jay is having car trouble and that he'll be there as soon as he can.

My story has more holes than a golf course, but car trouble is all I can come up with on the spur of the moment. As for Kate, I explain that she's still dealing with the investigators who are trolling all over Wally's and that she, too, will arrive at the hospital when she can.

Leaving my father again is more than difficult. I know it surprises him when I hug him and when I won't let go, but I can't help myself. His arms wrapped around me are what I need before I head off into battle.

And into battle is exactly where we're headed. Nathaniel isn't sure where Ariana is hiding, but he knows her well enough to point us in the right direction. Ariana likes the good life, he tells me, fine furnishings and people to cater to her, which is why he leads us to one of the finest hotels in town, The Sheraton Grand.

As Nathaniel is about to go charging into the lobby, Gage clasps his arm. "We can't just storm the place. We have to have a plan," he says.

"Because those have been working out really well for you," Nathaniel mocks.

A very stupid, possibly life-threatening, and certainly crazy thought comes to me. "I have an idea," I pipe in. "Let me go. Alone."

In unison they shout, "No!"

"Think about it," I say to them. "I'm who she wants. So why not offer a trade, me for them."

Again they yell, "No!"

"I don't see that we have much of a choice. We need a way to get inside and I'm it."

"It's suicide," Nathaniel barks.

Unexpectedly, Gage says, "It might work."

"Oh, good. You're both crazy." Nathaniel throws up his hands.

"It'll work if you take her in," Gage says to Nathaniel.

Nathanial guffaws at the idea. "Ariana and I aren't exactly on good terms these days."

"Use Mercy to get back in her good graces," Gage suggests.

Nathaniel considers the idea. While he does it gives me time to consider as well. What the hell am I thinking? Am I really ready to be reunited with my mother? The last time I saw her I was ten years old. I waved good-bye to her as she dropped me off at school. We arrived late after having spent the morning shopping together. The temperature outside was unbearable. Even with my hair pulled into a ponytail, sweat trickled down my neck. A damp ring accumulated on the back of my shirt where my book-laden backpack pressed into me.

She rolled down the window and called out to me, "Bye, Mercy. Love you!"

I can still picture her so clearly. Her red lipstick made the perfect frame for her beautiful smile. Her hair hung loosely around her shoulders. When she waved the bangles on her arm clanked together like wind chimes. Unfortunately, even after all these years, those are the only details of that moment I can remember. What happened after she pulled away from the curb remains a mystery.

The police never found her body. It was two years after she disappeared that they found her car at the bottom of the reservoir. She was presumed dead.

Clearly, we were wrong.

Chapter Twenty-Five

Gage

Ariana is supposed to be dead. She deceived me, and I don't know how. I have no alternative but to send Mercy in to gather information. But the ache gnawing at my stomach is making me apprehensive about the plan.

Nathaniel ushers me away from Mercy and whispers so that only I can hear. "I won't let anything happen to her," he tells me.

Going nearly nose-to-nose with Nathaniel, I say in my most authoritative voice, "Nothing about this is right. Putting my trust in you?"

"I don't see that you have any other choice," Nathaniel reminds me.

"If you cross me or if harm comes to her in any way, I swear ... "

Nathaniel narrows his eyes and chuckles, "You've really got it bad, don't you? That thing you feel, that drive at the pit of your stomach to stop at nothing. That pulsating in your chest when you look at her, or worse, when she's gone … "

"Shut up. Don't say anymore."

Mercy's cheeks redden and she turns away.

"Well, well, isn't this fun?" He claps my shoulders. "A Hunter in love with a human. I wonder what The Assembled will say about that."

I attempt to regain control of my emotions. "We don't have time for this, Nathaniel."

"Do you know how I know all of this, brother?" He says *brother* like it repulses him. "I know all of this because we are connected. You've chased me all over this world and yet, you've never been able to pull the trigger. Ever asked yourself why?"

"Shut up."

"Because your precious Assembled designed it that way. You blindly take orders and carry out their missions, but still you wonder why, don't you? Why would they connect you to me, link us in such a way?"

"I said, shut up!" I roar.

"Could it possibly be so that when I die, you die? Two birds. One stone."

No! It can't be true. I won't accept that.

Nathaniel presses on, saying, "It's why you let me live, why you pretend to study me, question my motives. You're delaying the inevitable. Self-preservation, just like the rest of us."

Nathaniel's words slice through me like shrapnel. Exposed, raw, every nerve in my body ignites and throbs. He's accusing me of being no better than him. But I'm nothing like him. I would never kill another for my own gain, for my own selfish reasons. The mere idea is in direct contradiction to everything I know about myself.

Before I have time to argue, before I have time to think, two men step out of the shadows.

"Mercy! Run!"

Chapter Twenty-Six

Mercy

No matter how fast I run, they gain. Fear turns to terror as a hand grabs the back of my neck. With a sure grip my pursuer tackles me to the hard ground. I yelp as the weight of him comes crashing down on top of me. He flips me over easily and mounts me, his knees pinning my arms to the ground. From his pocket he withdraws a long, gold-sheathed knife. I open my mouth to scream as he raises the blade, preparing to strike, but the pressure on my chest muffles any sound.

Suddenly he slumps forward. The knife flies out of his hand. I roll free and spring to my feet as Nathaniel pounces on him. With expertise, Nathaniel kicks him square in the chin. Blood and teeth spurt from his mouth.

Gage takes care of the partner. He slides up behind him, lassoes a chokehold around him and in one swift motion snaps his neck.

Nathaniel, however, likes to take his time. Much like my

attacker did to me, Nathaniel mounts him and delivers punch after punch until the thug's face resembles ground beef.

"Nathaniel!" Gage barks.

Disappointed that Gage interrupted him, Nathaniel rises to his feet. With the heel of his shoe he stamps the life from the motionless man. The crack of his neck echoes with a sickening crunch.

I expect to start shaking, to feel the heat intensify as my body prepares to breach. But I feel nothing. And that scares me even more. The idea that I am becoming accustomed to violence and death is unsettling.

"We need to get rid of the bodies," Nathaniel says matter-of-factly.

I scan the street. "There's a dumpster in the alley." I point.

Nathaniel grins, his left eyebrow dancing. "You catch on quick."

A sickening shiver ripples my spine. I swallow hard to force down what I'm feeling.

Gage steps between us. "Help me." He grunts as he lifts the heavier of the two.

Running ahead of them I prop open the dumpster lid. Together, Gage and Nathaniel heave the body into the trash.

"One down, one to go," Nathaniel remarks.

"Human life really means that little to you, doesn't it?" I snap.

"I just saved your ass," he points out. "Save the lecture."

Shut down, frustrated, and tired, I wait by the dumpster as Gage and Nathaniel retrieve the other body.

The night air creeps in and shivers work their way across my skin. Rubbing my arms to keep warm, I move away from the stench of the dumpster when a hand reaches out and covers my mouth.

No chance to scream, no chance to run, the last thing I see before the syringe pierces my skin is the clear, night sky.

My eyelids fight against sleep and lose. In my dreams I see Lyla, sitting on her porch, painting her toenails a ridiculous shade of red. She waves me over.

"You have that look on your face," she says coolly.

"What look?"

"That stick-up-your-butt look."

"What? I do not!"

She brushes the polish onto her toes, not looking up at me. "You never want to have any fun."

"That's not true," I protest.

"Sure it is," she says, still not looking up at me. "That's why no one wants to date you and you don't have any friends besides me."

Taken aback and unable to hide the look of hurt on my face, I say, rather snidely, "Gee, Lyla, why don't you tell me how you really feel."

She looks up at me, her head cocked oddly, almost demon-like. "You hate me, don't you?" Methodically, she rises from the porch, the nail polish tipping over and spilling a thick river of red down the steps. "You're going to kill me." Suddenly she has a knife in her hand and she waves it at me. "Go ahead."

Backing away from the blade I retreat across the lawn. "Lyla, put the knife down. I don't want to kill you."

With the knife in her right hand, Lyla holds out her left forearm. The tip of the blade edges along her skin, slicing just deep enough for trickles of blood to leak.

"Lyla! Stop!"

"You know this is what you want. You want me dead. Then

you'll be free." She slices another line in her skin.

"Stop!" I yell.

"Come on, Mercy." She wields the knife, skillfully, purposefully, as she digs into her shoulder. More blood, so much more blood escapes, wetting her shirt.

"Please." I stumble and hit the ground. She towers over me, holding the knife to her throat. "Lyla! Don't!"

I lunge for the knife, but not in time. Lyla drags the blade across her throat. Thick sprays of crimson spew forth covering my face.

I wake to the sound of my own screaming.

Tears gather in the corners of my eyes and dribble down my cheeks. It's useless to wipe them because they relentlessly keep on coming.

Lyla. Lyla. Lyla. What have I done?

She's gone and it's entirely my fault. She was my friend. Is my friend! She *is* my friend and I did this to her. I took away her life and for that I will never forgive myself.

Gage says this isn't my fault. Nathaniel says this isn't my fault. But I know the truth. I am a Breacher. I am a lowlife, soul-sucking Breacher who doesn't deserve to live, just like Rae said.

I should end this. It's wrong to go on living in Lyla's body. It's selfish. I keep telling myself that I can't kill her, that I'm not the kind of person who kills my friend, but Nathaniel is right. I already did.

The minute I took her body I killed her. I'm deluding myself that the only reason I haven't left her body yet is because I can't bring myself to end her life. Her life is already over. She's gone and I'm tired of being selfish.

It's time to set Lyla free. But first I have to figure out where the hell I am.

The cot I woke up on is pushed against a dingy, paint-chipped wall in a room the size of a cell. In the corner there's a hole in the floor. Silently, I pray that I won't have to use it.

The locked door at the end of the room has the tiniest of windows. I strain to see right or left, but can make out only darkness. Returning to the cot, I sit back down. There's nothing left to do but wait.

When the door finally opens, the face that greets me is not the one I'd been expecting.

"Rae?"

"Not exactly."

"I don't understand. What's going on?" I press myself against the wall as she comes further into the room. "Where's Gage?"

Her eyes flicker with recognition, but there's no love in her expression. Something is different. This is not the Rae I know.

"Such a delicious choice, isn't it? Gage? Nathaniel?" She strums her fingertips together. "Whomever will you choose?"

Everything pulls into focus and my heart sinks. This isn't Rae. Yes, she looks just like her, but it isn't her. And then I understand. She's a replica, a sister, a copy of the original, only evil.

"Son of a bitch!" I yell.

Tilting her head to the side she says, "A little slow to catch on, don't you think?"

"Why? You didn't have to kill her!"

"I never have to do anything. But I'm allowed to have a little fun."

"Fun? You're sick." All the fear I feel is replaced with rage, steaming, violent rage.

I fly at her, grab her neck and squeeze until my fingers scream in pain. She struggles against me, claws at my hands. It's a natural reaction that any human being would have. But this is no *human* being. After a momentary struggle, she lets go and smiles.

The smile on her face is wrong. All wrong. I let go.

Chapter Twenty-Seven

Gage

With the second body evenly distributed between us, Nathaniel and I lug it over to the dumpster when suddenly he halts.

"Where's Mercy?" he asks.

My head whips around, hoping for any sign of her, but she's nowhere to be found.

As quickly as we can, we load the second body into the dumpster. Blood stains our hands and clothes. Normally, I'd worry that someone might spot us and alert the police, but I can't think about that now. My focus is solely on Mercy.

"Look!" I point to the ground near the dumpster. Nathaniel follows my gaze until he, too, stares at the needle on the ground.

Carefully he picks it up and examines it. "They took her."

With that realization, I lose it. Kicking and punching at the dumpster, I wail out my aggression. I don't know if I'm shouting anything coherent or intelligible, it's more like the ravings of a madman.

Mercy. They took Mercy. My hands shake. I clench and unclench my fists as my heart pounds against my ribs. I bit my lip to keep it from quivering. I am unraveling. How did this happen to me? How did I go from steeled Hunter to this?

Everything I feel is so *human*. It's stupid to keep on denying it. I have feelings for her. I worry about her. I may even love … No. I can't think about that now.

Nathaniel hasn't said anything during my temper tantrum, which I appreciate. His sarcastic comments are not what I need right now.

"What's the plan?" he finally asks me.

For the first time ever, I don't know.

"Gage, we can't stand around all day kicking dumpsters. We have to figure out a way to get in there."

"There's only one way."

Nathaniel catches on quick, the smirk he wears tells me he knows exactly what I'm thinking.

Nathaniel claps me on the back. "This is going to be fun."

We make our way to the hotel. The lobby is bustling, which is ideal for slipping in unnoticed. Nathaniel surveys the surroundings. Hanging back a bit, I take a good look around. Nothing appears out of place. There's zero indication that something disturbing is going on.

After a short wait in line it's my turn to approach the front desk.

"I'm looking for Ariana White," I inform the woman. "She's expecting me."

Typing into her computer the woman furrows her brow and says, "I'm sorry, sir, there's no one here by that name."

Figures. "Try Molly Sherman or Molly Sherman Clare."

Again, her fingernails tap against the keys, the faint clicking sound grates my nerves as my impatience grows.

"Here we are," she says. "Penthouse suite. I'll have to call ahead. There's a notice that she's not to be disturbed."

"No need," I say. "I'll try again another time."

"Would you care to leave a message?"

The thought crosses my mind to leave some cryptic message, but it's better to keep the element of surprise on our side. "No message, thank you."

Nathaniel is waiting for me in the bar. I sit down next to him and watch him down a tumbler of whiskey.

"She's in the penthouse suite," I tell him.

He responds with, "Of course."

My thumb raps against the rail of the bar. Nathaniel reaches over and holds it down.

"Stop. Your agitation is annoying me."

"Yeah, well, your lack of agitation is annoying me. This has to work or we're going to be in a serious trouble."

"I know what's at stake, Gage. You don't need to keep reminding me."

"You've known Ariana was alive this whole time, haven't you?"

Nathaniel's grudgingly nods.

"And you knew she'd come for Mercy?"

He nods again.

"You came to protect Mercy, didn't you?"

Nathaniel rotates toward me slowly. "Yes, I did."

I know I should stop there, that I don't need to hear the rest, but I can't stop. "Because you love her." It isn't a question.

"Just like you. Let's go," Nathaniel says, breaking my concentration.

In one smooth motion, Nathaniel slides off the barstool and stalks out the room. With purpose he crosses the lobby and sidles up closely, but not too closely, behind a twenty-something bellhop.

The bellhop is of average height, but more muscular than most. He works out, evident by the way the fabric of his shirt strains as he walks.

Nathaniel's mark is no pushover. It won't be easy to take him down.

The bellhop glances over his shoulder at us as we follow him into the elevator bank. He's nonchalant about it, but I know we've raised his suspicion.

When the elevator dings, announcing its arrival, we three huddle together as the car empties. Once inside, the bellhop motions to us and asks, "Floor?"

"The penthouse," Nathaniel replies.

The bellhop turns his back to us again and that's when Nathaniel pounces.

He's not as unsuspecting as we would like. He fights back, giving Nathaniel a run for his money. He almost knocks Nathaniel out. I have to step in and get my hands dirty. It isn't long before Nathaniel and I pin him down.

He struggles against us and I start to lose my grip. "Hurry up," I shout to Nathaniel.

Nathaniel's breathing intensifies and his face contorts right before he shatters into a million pieces. The blast blows me back against the elevator wall. I lose my hold on the bellhop. Fortunately for us, he's too stunned to move.

The pieces of Nathaniel swarm and then dive into the open mouth of the horrified bellhop. His entire body goes rigid and then convulses. Flopping around on the elevator floor, he flips from his back to his stomach and then he is motionless.

He stays still for too long. Then, slowly, he pushes himself up into a standing position.

"Nathaniel?"

He stretches and flexes his muscles down to his fingertips then cracks his neck. "It's a bit snug, but it'll do."

What we're doing is wrong. So wrong. It goes against everything I've ever been taught, against everything I've ever known or believed. I'm aiding and abetting in a breach. Have I really come to this? Have I sunk this low?

Yes, I have. The evidence is right in front of me.

But there's no turning back now. We've already gone too far over the edge to try scrambling back up the cliff. Since there's no retreating, the only choice is to move forward.

The elevator stops at the top floor.

"Tenth floor. Women's lingerie," Nathaniel jokes.

I grab his arm. "Just surveillance, Nathaniel. Don't do anything stupid."

"Who, me?"

Nathaniel and I are two steps away from the elevator when the penthouse door flings open and two men followed by a woman come running toward us. Nathaniel is quick to react and he yanks me back into the elevator. Pushing the door close button over and over I pray that the door closes before they get to us.

It does.

"What was that?"

"Something's wrong," Nathaniel answers.

Chapter Twenty-Eight

Mercy

My insides pull in different directions, trying to rip me apart. Sweat accumulates and trickles, then gushes from beneath Lyla's thick hair and down her back. Her heart pounds and pounds like a bass drum. I curl into a ball and will myself together.

The pain comes in waves and then in jolts, stabbing, scorching, until every nerve screams in agony. The sounds that come from me are from a place deep inside. I don't even know how I'm creating them.

All I want is for it to end.

And so it does.

But what follows is much worse.

I'm no longer on the cot. I'm across the room, standing over the hole in the floor. Lyla's body is motionless on the bed.

Oh God. What have I done?

Looking down at myself I see that I'm transparent,

practically see-through, like a ghost. I'm wearing the gray dress that Lyla picked out for my birthday party. It's what I was wearing the night that I supposedly died. My hands, my skin, my legs and feet, they're all there and yet not there.

Cautiously, I move toward Lyla, my feet never quite connecting to the ground. She still isn't moving. Reaching out, I try to feel a pulse, but my hand goes through her wrist and I yank it back.

Lyla, I'm so sorry.

I thought I'd spoken the words out loud, but my voice is only in my head.

Moving away from the cot, I let my legs fold underneath me and I sit on the floor. It feels like sitting, I know there's something hard beneath me, but at the same time I can't feel the actual floor.

Does it really matter? I wonder. *Does how I feel mean anything anymore? No. Not after what I'd done.*

Until this moment, I'd hoped that maybe Gage and Nathaniel and everyone else were wrong about me and about Breachers. Until this moment I'd believed that maybe I was different and that there was a way to save Lyla. I was wrong.

Slowly, I let go of all hope and let the guilt take root. I want to cry and mourn forever.

Lyla's hand twitches. I think maybe I'd imagined it, but then her foot moves slightly and she moans.

Lyla!

I yell and yell, but she can't hear me.

"My head." Her voice is scratchy, raw. She closes her eyes and her head lolls, but I can see her chest rise and fall. She's breathing.

Lyla? Can you hear me?

Sluggishly, she rolls over to her side and then pushes herself into a sitting position. She moves like her body weighs a metric ton. Helpless, I watch as she struggles.

She isn't dead. I haven't killed her. I want to rejoice with her, to hug her and squeeze her and apologize until I'm hoarse, but I can't do any of that.

Lyla must be scared out of her mind, not to mention confused or possibly hurt, and there's nothing I can do to help her.

"Worst hangover ever," Lyla mumbles.

Not a hangover! Lyla, look around. You're in a cell. You're in danger.

Almost as if she hears me, Lyla looks around. She squints as though the light hurts her eyes. Rubbing her temples she lifts her head all the way and the look on her face tells me that she's finally starting to realize that something is very wrong.

"Where am I?"

Scrambling back onto the cot until she's flattened against the wall, like she did when she was little, Lyla jams her fists into her eye sockets and hums a little tune.

I'm so sorry for all of this, Lyla. I wish I could help you, explain to you what's happening.

Lyla drags herself off the cot and edges along the wall to the door. She tries the handle only to find it locked. "Hey, let me out," she yells. Pulling harder she yanks the door, but it won't budge. "Let me out!" she yells again.

Letting go of the door, Lyla looks around the room again. Panic washes over her face. She backs herself into the door, spins around and starts pounding. "Help! Somebody help me!" She bangs and bangs until her hand is red.

With her cheek against the door, Lyla begins to cry. "Please.

Please don't leave me in here."

The lock on the door clicks. Scared, Lyla backs away. She backs right through me and I gasp. The door opens and Jay, held by two large men, stumbles in.

"Jay!" Lyla rushes for him just as the men let go. He looks like he's going to fall, but Lyla catches him.

The weight of him against her nearly overtakes her, but Lyla's strong. She half carries him over to the cot and lowers him down. Jay sits slumped against the wall as Lyla checks him over.

"Jay, are you hurt? What's happening? Where are we?" She holds his face in her hands. The bruise that surrounds his left eye is rapidly swelling and darkening in color. His lip is cut and caked with blood, as is his left nostril. He's taken a beating.

"Jay," Lyla tries again. "Talk to me, please."

"Mercy," he whispers.

Oh no.

"Jay?"

Jay closes his eyes and rests his head against the wall. He holds up his hand and says, "Just give me a sec."

Lyla waits, wiping her face of tears. She's not a patient person and I can see her need for answers building. "Who did this to you?" she asks. "What happened? I can't remember anything. Why can't I remember?"

Jay grunts as he moves himself into a more upright position. His left eye barely opens, and he grimaces when he runs his fingers along the welted skin.

"Jay, I'm scared," Lyla says.

"We're gonna be okay," he says to reassure her.

"Do you know where we are?" she asks.

"Yeah." He shifts positions. "It's the old meat packing plant in midtown."

"How did we get here?"

Jay shakes his head, like he's trying to rattle the memory loose. "I was at home, watching TV and I heard my mom scream. I ran down the hall and then I saw … " His voice trails off.

Lyla gasps. "Oh, my God! Is she okay?"

Jay shakes his head again, swallows hard. He says through clenched teeth, "I don't know. Someone hit me from behind and I woke up tied to a chair in a room with one light hanging from the ceiling like in some freaking gangster movie or something."

"I don't understand."

"It's your mother," Jay starts. "She's here. At first I didn't want to believe it because she's dead, but she knew things and … " He doesn't finish.

Lyla looks shocked. "My mom?"

"It was freaky. She kept asking me all these questions about you and Gage. She wanted to know everything he told you."

"Gage? But that doesn't make sense. None of this makes sense. My mom is dead. We buried her. I was there. I watched her body go into the ground."

That's right, Ly. We buried your mom. But we didn't bury mine.

"Mercy, your mother's body was never found. She's here. And she's pissed."

"It must be your head. You're so confused."

"I'm not confused. Your mom is very much alive and I know you don't want to believe me, but it's true, Mercy. Your mother is the reason we're in this mess."

Lyla freezes. "Jay, I'm not Mercy. I'm Lyla, can't you see that?"

Jay scoots forward and stands to his full height. "Are you playing some type of game? Cuz it's not fucking funny."

"I'm not playing any game. Why would I do that?"

Jay grabs Lyla forcefully and shakes her. "Who are you? What have you done with Mercy?"

"Jay, let go. You're hurting me." Lyla squirms beneath his grasp.

He releases his grip and eyes her skeptically. "What's going on?"

"I don't know," Lyla starts. "Something's wrong with you."

"Who are you?"

"Jay, it's me, Lyla." Her voice breaks ever so slightly when she says, "Don't you know me?"

Jay doesn't know what to think or what to believe. This is too much for him. I can see it. He's near to breaking.

I wish I could tell him, help him see that his girlfriend, who he thought he lost, is standing right in front of him.

Lyla puts both her hands on Jay's chest and she kisses him beneath his chin. His eyes close and his body tenses. "Jay," she whispers against his throat. "Please come back to me."

Chapter Twenty-Nine

Gage

We ride the elevator down to the lobby. By the time we get there, there's no sign of Ariana's men. A quick search reveals no clues as to which way they've gone or why they've run out in such a hurry.

"Hey, Darren," a cute girl with blond curls and a sweet smile calls out to us. "Jim says there's a backload at the curb and he wants you out there."

Nathaniel and I look at each other. He responds, "Well, Jim's going to have to wait."

"Rude. What's with you?"

"Headache," Nathaniel tells her. "I'm going home."

We head toward the exit.

"So, will I see you later?" she calls after him.

"Probably on the news," Nathaniel quips at a volume only he and I can hear.

Once outside, we take off down the street and turn the corner.

Sacramento's midtown is full of alleys, plenty of places to duck into and take cover. Soon, Nathaniel and I are out of sight.

Nathaniel begins rooting around.

"What are you doing?" I ask him.

"I'm looking for something sharp, like a glass bottle. Be useful and help me."

This is the part of our plan that I dread, the part where we dispose of Darren. The internal conflict is undeniable, but there isn't time to dwell so I help Nathaniel until eventually we find what we're looking for.

"Here." I hand him an empty beer bottle.

"I thought for sure you'd want to do the honors."

"Just do it and get it over with."

Nathaniel bashes the bottle against the side of the building, breaking it in half. Jagged edged and sharp, the bottle is now a weapon. Nathaniel uses it to end the life of Darren the bellhop.

The body falls to the ground and I drag it into the nearby bushes, concealing it the best I can. While I hide the evidence, Nathaniel returns to form.

"We have to figure out what happened," I say, not necessarily to Nathaniel, but to myself as well.

"I don't think it's that difficult to figure out," Nathaniel says flatly.

"What do you mean?"

"Put the pieces together, Gage. They lost Mercy. Or Mercy escaped. Either way, she's out in the wild."

"By escaped you mean … " I can't finish the sentence.

Nathaniel finishes it for me. "She jumped? That's exactly what I mean. If she was scared enough, or hurt, it's a definite possibility."

He's probably right. It makes sense. It also means that by

now The Assembled might know that Mercy didn't kill Lyla when she left her body. And if that's true, Mercy is in more danger than ever before.

Breachers are impulsive and reckless by nature. Mercy, full of grief and remorse, is like a ticking time bomb. She won't know what's happening to her or how to stop and she could end up anywhere, in anyone. We have to find her. Fast.

"Do you think any of your fancy Breacher tracker equipment still works?" Nathaniel asks me.

Jinx. I'd give anything to be able to talk to Jinx, but I can't think about that right now. As for the equipment, if there isn't too much smoke or water damage, it's possible. There's a shred of hope.

If Nathaniel is wrong and Mercy hasn't left Lyla's body, we'll only be wasting time returning to the warehouse. But there's nothing else to go on so we take off running.

The wreckage is sickening. It's no longer a safe haven. It's been violated in the worst way. The fire trucks have come and gone, though investigators still linger. We have to sneak inside.

The halls are underneath an inch of water. The walls are scorched and sagging. Jinx's body is still in his chair. It's possible the investigators haven't found it yet, or they'd found it and are waiting for the Crime Scene Units. Either way, they'll be returning which means we're under a time crunch.

Parts of the control panel are fried, but all is not lost. A few of the monitors are still working. I move around Jinx, careful not to disturb his body. Though I'm schooled in how to work the controls of the Observation Deck, I'm not schooled in its repair. I quickly begin to lose hope and my patience.

"This is useless!" I yell, slamming my hand down on the board. I watch with surprise as the keys light up.

Working as quickly as I can, I punch in the codes and wait for the screens to show us something, anything.

Two minutes, five minutes, ten minutes. Nothing.

"She could be anywhere." Frustration rings in my voice.

"Someone's coming." Nathaniel motions toward the door.

Quickly we dash out of sight. Giving each other hand signals we communicate our next move. I move to the left so that I can circle back and sneak up on whoever it is while Nathaniel chooses the frontal attack. Duck-walking my way around the room I spy two sets of feet, which I signal to Nathaniel.

On his count, we pounce.

Using my crouched position, I sweep the legs of the attacker closest to me. Nathaniel dives at the other guy. With surprise on our side, we subdue the two men without much effort. Nathaniel continues to kick the guy about the ribs until blood bubbles from his mouth.

"Enough! He's no good to us dead."

Nathaniel spits in his face and leaves him to wail and clench his middle section.

"One of you gets to be our guest and tell us everything we want to know." Nathaniel stands authoritatively over them both. "The other gets to die. You let me know what you decide."

"I'll tell you nothing," the guy Nathaniel kicked croaks out.

"Works for me," Nathaniel says and then he stomps the guy's face in. He turns to the other and says, "Looks like you get to talk."

I pull him to his feet and hold him against the wall. "You work for Ariana?"

He nods.

"Where's Mercy?"

He doesn't answer. "I think he needs some encouragement," I say to Nathaniel.

Nathaniel approaches, but he doesn't have to strike. The guy starts singing.

"We lost her. Ariana sent us here to find her," he says. "She told us about your machine and how it tracks Breachers."

Son of a bitch! Nathaniel is right. Mercy is no longer in Lyla's body.

"Where are Jay and Kate?"

He hesitates, so I punch him in the gut. Seizing him by the throat I hold him against the wall.

"Where are Jay and Kate?"

"Ariana has them."

"They're not at the hotel, are they?" Nathaniel asks. "Where is she keeping them?"

Again, he stays quiet longer than I'm willing to tolerate so I knee him in the groin. That gets him talking.

"Meat. Packing. Plant," he says between gasps for air.

"And Rae? Is she there too?"

He shakes his head.

"Where is she?"

"Dead."

With that I let him fall to the floor. Nathaniel kicks him about the head until he falls unconscious.

Rae is dead? That can't be. It isn't possible that I lost my entire team in one day.

What is my purpose in all of this? I'm not even sure who I'm fighting for or why. Is Nathaniel still my enemy? Will we turn on each other once we have Mercy back? I have no idea what my future holds.

"You go to the meat packing plant," Nathaniel says. "I'll stay here and see if I can find Mercy."

Nathaniel giving me orders isn't exactly sitting well with me. Too much is happening and I'm unequipped to handle any of it.

"My team is dead."

I don't realize I said it out loud until Nathaniel responds.

"Now is not the time to go all human on me, Gage. We haven't failed until Mercy is dead and she's not dead. She's out there alone and we need to find her. We can deal with everything else later."

Nathaniel is right. Best not to think too far ahead.

"Go to the meat packing plant. Get Jay and Kate and meet me back here."

"Okay. But first we need armor."

The weapons room is at the end of the hall and down a narrow staircase. It's unfortunate I have to knock out a fire investigator along the way, but there's no time to think, only to act.

"This is an extractor." I hand Nathaniel a tool that to the untrained eye resembles a stun gun. "Point and shoot, pretty self-explanatory."

Nathaniel gives me a wry smile. "I'm familiar."

"Right."

We load up with guns, knives, and whatever we can find. I toss Nathaniel an equipment vest and we spend a few minutes strapping down all that we have collected.

"Are you sure you're going to be able to find Mercy?" I ask him.

"No."

His answer isn't exactly confidence inspiring.

Equipped with all the weapons I need, I leave Nathaniel at

The Observation Deck and make my way out of the building. It would've been faster to drive to the meat packing plant, but I can't risk a trip to the garage to get a car.

I double-time it on foot, stopping short about a block and a half away. The street is quiet, too quiet, which means that Ariana has lookouts. From my breast pocket I withdraw a pair of binoculars and scan the area. Sure enough, there are men stationed at all the exits. There are two men in a car across the street and one on the roof of the opposite building.

I take the roof out first. Climbing the side ladder, I use the silencer and drop him without breaking a sweat. The two in the car are next. Once they're out of the way, my path to the guards at the door is free.

I used the .45 and both go down without ever getting a shot at me. Once the Breachers find new bodies, they'll be back, but at least I've bought myself some time.

The meat packing plant is cold, though I expect the freezers haven't been used in years. It's dark inside and the floor is stained with animal blood. Hooks hang from the ceilings. Retired machines idle, rusting from lack of use.

Slithering through the building, I come upon a lone woman who looks as though she's waiting for me.

"You're good," she remarks. "I'm better."

Quicker than I expect she draws her weapon and fires. Ducking and rolling to my right I keep moving until the spray of bullets cease. I can tell from her footsteps that she's approaching. When she's within range, she starts firing again.

Running as fast as I can, I take cover behind a table. When I know she's near, I return fire. She ducks behind a pillar and waits for me to give up.

Empty, I throw my gun to the ground and reach for a knife.

Flinging it in her direction, it grazes her shoulder, ripping her white blouse. She reaches down and wipes the blood from her arm.

"Lucky shot."

I throw another knife and this time I hit her square in the throat. She clutches at it, but it's too deep to remove. Within seconds she's dead.

The double knife throw. I learned that from Zee. Even in death, he's still saving my life.

In the clear, I begin a room-to-room search. It's in the third room that I find Rae.

Her beautiful blond hair is matted and caked with blood. Her legs are bent in the same direction. Had there not been a puddle of sticky, red blood, I might have been able to imagine that she was sleeping. Kneeling beside her body, I take her hand in mine. She's cold and stiff.

My Rae. Gone.

I kiss her fingertips and grope along her arm, wishing for the warmth that used to radiate from her.

Finding Zee, finding Jinx, it was nothing like this. There's an ache in my chest that I've never experienced before, like my insides are wringing themselves out. The back of my throat tightens and clenches making it difficult to swallow. My lips tremble slightly and, for the first time since I was created, I cry.

With my free hand, I touch my face and feel the wetness, the manifestation of sorrow. Following the grief is a surge of emotions, one piled on top of the other without rhyme or reason. Hatred, anger, revenge, guilt, sadness, it's all there, swirling inside me and bubbling forth.

"I'm so sorry," I cry to her. "I will find who did this to you, Rae, that I swear."

Chapter Thirty

Mercy

"Lyla, is that really you?" Jay's voice is full of hope.

Gunshots. Lyla and Jay jump, fumble closer together, and huddle against the wall.

"What's happening?" Lyla asks, her voice nearing hysteria.

"I don't know." Jay pulls Lyla into a protective grasp.

More gunshots, and then it's over. All that's left is an eerie silence. Lyla and Jay continue staring at the door waiting for it to open, bracing themselves for whatever horror lies beyond, but nothing happens.

After a few moments, Jay parts from Lyla just a bit. He brushes the hair back from her shoulders and inspects every inch of her face. His hands rest on the sides of her neck, his thumb brushing the line of her jaw. Tentatively, he leans in, but only halfway.

Lyla puts her hands on his waist, tugging slightly at the bottom of his shirt. She tilts her head to the right and waits for him to pull her in.

It's the moment before the kiss, when the anticipation builds and the heart races and the pulse quickens, because both people know what's about to happen. I'm watching Lyla and Jay have that moment. They've found their way back to each other.

I don't watch them kiss. Hearing it is enough and it isn't my moment to share. I try as best I can to give them privacy.

When I hear Jay say, "I thought I lost you," I turn back around.

"You found me," she responds.

Jay takes Lyla by the hand and leads her to the cot. He sits her down next to him and says, "There's something I have to tell you."

He's going to try and explain to her about me. He's going to tell her what I've done, that I took her body and nearly killed her. Breath escapes me as I wait for him to tell her of all the things I've done.

"It's about Mercy," he continues.

Lyla sucks in a breath then says, "I remember. The birthday party, the alley, it's foggy, but it's there. Mercy had like a seizure or something right? Is she okay?"

Shaking his head slightly, Jay says, "No, she's not okay. Ly, this is going to be really weird and messed up, and I swear I wouldn't have believed it myself, but after everything that's happened … "

Lyla interrupts him by saying, "Just tell me."

"Um, well," he stammers. "Um, when we got to the hospital, you were acting really weird."

"I was at the hospital? I don't remember that."

"Right, because it wasn't really you. I mean it was you,

like you, you know?"

"I haven't heard you struggle this much since we had to recite Shakespeare in the seventh grade. Spit it out, you're killing me."

Oh, Ly, poor choice of words.

"Mercy was in your body."

Ka-boom. There it is, the ugly truth.

Lyla laughs a nervous laugh. "What?"

"It all has to do with her mom and Gage and believe me, I still don't understand it all, but somehow Mercy took over your body. And we thought, well, she told me that in order to get out, she'd have to kill you. She didn't want to do that so she stayed. But you're here, so she must've been wrong."

Lyla looks horrified. Both her mouth and her eyes are open wide. "Mercy was going to kill me?"

No! Lyla, that's not what I wanted!

"Did she try to kill me?" Lyla checks herself over.

"I don't know," Jay says. "I didn't even know she, well you, were here until they threw me in here."

"So, where is Mercy now?"

I'm right here! Why can't you hear me?

"Maybe she figured out a way to get out without having to kill you." Jay gestures toward Lyla and says, "Well, obviously she did because you're here and not dead and she's, man, I don't know."

"You realize this sounds insane?"

"Yep. But Ly, there's more."

Lyla gets up off the cot and walks a few feet away. She crosses her arms over her chest and poses in her stance of defiance, one hip cocked. "You know what, Jay, this is a lot to process and I'm not sure if I can take anymore." Lyla paces back and forth for a moment and then pivots to face Jay straight on. "We can't stay here. We have to do something."

That's the Lyla I know and love, the one who isn't afraid of anything, the one who's fiercely protective of the ones she loves.

"Like what? Ly, these people, these Breacher things, they're no joke. I've already seen Mercy ... " He pauses. "I know she didn't do that to you on purpose, but still, she can take bodies. All the Breachers can apparently. We need to be careful."

Hearing Jay express his fear of me is like taking a bullet to the chest. I'm a monster and he's right. My two best friends in the world have every reason to fear me.

Lyla, listening to Jay's words carefully, begins to put the pieces together. "Wait, you said before that Mercy's mother is alive. Is that true?"

"Yeah. Freaky, right?"

"Does Mercy know?"

"No idea. But I don't think it's going to be a happy reunion."

Lyla sits back down on the bed and sighs, and for the next few moments there's silence. How desperately I want to join them, to be near them and draw comfort from them. Mostly, I want to tell them how sorry I am for causing all of this.

Jay pulls Lyla into him and she nestles against his chest. At least they have each other.

Suddenly, the door bursts open and all of us jump.

Gage!

He's dressed in combat gear, a black vest, heavily equipped with weapons fits snugly to him. In his hand he holds some type of handgun, which he holsters immediately. His usually slicked hair is mussed, his cheeks flushed. His dark eyes are even darker, black and piercing.

A strange look comes across Gage's face and then he seizes Lyla and hugs her. "Mercy!"

Jay jumps up and tries to pry Gage off Lyla, but Gage will not let go.

"I thought … "

Lyla backs away. "I'm not Mercy."

Gage looks to Jay for an explanation, but Jay throws up his hands and says, "Don't look at me. I have no idea. I'm just as confused as you are."

"No," Gage starts.

"Uh, thanks," Lyla says in a hurt voice.

Gage's eyes dart back and forth. With his hands on his hips he says, "I didn't mean to imply … " He seems to be having difficultly thinking of the right words to say. "You're sure?"

"Oh yeah, I'm sure," Lyla says.

"And Mercy? Is she … ?"

Is she standing just a few feet from you? Yes! Why can't you see me? Gage! I begin to scream. *Gage!*

"Did you hear that?" Gage asks.

Holy shit! It's working. Gage!

"Hear what?" Lyla asks.

Gage concentrates, holds up a hand telling them to be quiet while he listens.

I'm here! I yell.

"What is it?" Jay asks.

Gage hesitates and then says, "I thought I heard … " He stops. "Never mind."

Don't give up! Gage!

"Mercy?"

He looks right at me when he speaks, steps in my direction

and I think maybe, just maybe, he can hear me.

Lyla and Jay look around the room and then back at Gage. I can tell they want to see what he's seeing, but they can't.

Can you see me?

"No, but I can hear you."

What's happening to me?

"Are you talking to her? Is Mercy here?" Lyla moves closer to Gage.

"I think so," Gage answers.

With all of my might I concentrate, throw my energy at Gage. It's a strange sensation, to say the least. It isn't like before, with all the pain. This time it's all heat, buzzing around me like a vortex and I thrust it at Gage.

Around me a light begins to glow.

"What is that?" Lyla asks.

Gage sounds stunned and thrilled when he says, "You can see it?"

I begin to fill in, to take shape, but I'm still not whole. It's more like an image of me. Looking my hands over, mesmerized by what's happening, I almost forget that they're in the room with me.

Then Gage says, "Mercy, I can see you."

Nodding, smiling, I let out a laugh mixed with surprise. It's overwhelming to no longer be alone. Gage reaches out a hand to me and I reciprocate. Unlike before, when I couldn't feel anything, I tingle when Gage touches me. It isn't much, but at least it's something.

His eyes well with tears and so do mine. Knowing he can feel me means everything. It fills me up completely, even if I am, physically, only an image of myself.

"Can you hear me?" I ask.

"Yes, but just barely."

"Gage, am I dead?" More tears as he tries to squeeze my hand and it slides through me instead of connecting with me.

He looks pained, which makes me want to touch him even more.

"I'll fix this," he swears to me. "I promise."

I attempt a grin, but my lips falter and quiver. Looking over at Lyla and Jay, at their sweet faces, which are also wet with tears, I know I have to keep it together, for them. Being in this whole mess is my fault. I've done this to them. Maybe it's better if I'm dead.

"Mercy! What's happening?" Gage lunges toward me as I flicker in and out.

Losing my grip, my image falters and I feel myself slipping away. Despite my efforts to hang on, I can't fight it. It's too much for me.

"Do something!" Lyla yells at Gage.

But what can he do?

A force grips me and spins me and the last thing I hear is Gage shouting my name.

Chapter Thirty-One

I land hard. The wind knocks out of me. I suck in air, but I can't breathe. I feel the weight of someone on top of me, smothering me. My lungs struggle, finding no relief. I hear a gurgling sound, like bubbling water. I realize quickly the awful noise is actually coming from me. I'm in someone's body. *Shit!*

I realize I can't breathe. Something is covering my face. A pillow. I try to suck in air, but I only get a mouthful of fabric. Panic swells within me. The sound of my throbbing heart, pumping furiously, drums wildly in my ears.

I squirm. I writhe. I buck like a bronco forcing the weight off of me. A man grunts, and mashes the pillow deeper into my face. I feel my nose crack and my eyes bulge. Time is running out. With all my strength I shove him off. He jumps back off the bed, startled by my sudden burst. He scrambles against the wall, stumbling as he goes. He stares at me, his mouth agape with horror. His eyes are wide, truly terrified. Of me.

He runs faster than anyone I have ever seen.

When I feel calm, I look at the room around me. The walls are painted slate blue. Pictures of beach scenes hang in white frames. There's a vase of daisies on the dresser. The sheets on the bed are mussed. The room feels disturbed. Remnants of the intruder hang heavy in the air; the smell of his sweat is musky and lingering.

I exit the bedroom and walk down a short hall. These walls are covered in pictures as well. But instead of beach scenes there are smiling faces. College parties, groups of girls with their arms around each other raising their beers in toast. Children at the zoo, poking their heads through cutouts of Gorillas. An old fashioned photo of a couple getting married. The faces are pleasant and somehow welcoming, yet entirely foreign to me.

The hall spills out into a cozy family room with worn couches. An aged wooden table is centered on a blue and cream rug. Atop the table lies People magazine, US Weekly, and yesterday's paper. I try not to stare too hard at the date. It's inconceivable to me that a few days ago I was an average girl. It's difficult to believe what I've become in such a short time.

I continue through the living room and end up in the kitchen. The cupboards are antique white. A wall clock in the shape of a rooster lets me know it's ten fifteen PM.

I have the urge to splash some water on my face. I set off in search of the powder room, which I find at the end of the hall. Flipping on the light, I see that everything is pink, like a gumball exploded. Looking up in the mirror, I suck in a breath when I see my reflection.

The hair is short, pixie cut, and black as night. The eyes

are almond shaped and the irises are dark and murky. The skin is pale, almost translucent, like non-fat milk. She's shorter than me. I touch her face. Her skin is cold, well below room temperature.

Not only am I in another body, I'm in someone else's dead body. I can see it in the broken blood vessels around the eyeballs, the chalky blue of the lips.

It makes sense now, my attacker's reaction. He thought she came back from the dead. She did—in a way.

This is bad. This is very, very bad.

"You're prettier than she is," Nathaniel says from behind me.

My eyes catch his reflection in the mirror. I flinch and spin around to face him.

I scream at him. "I'm in a dead body!"

"And whose fault is that?" He gives me a stern look.

Like a child, I stomp my foot, her foot. "Help me!"

He sighs. "Follow me." Nathaniel spins on his heels and walks, noiselessly, down the hall.

At the door to the bedroom, he pauses and then turns abruptly. I stop just before slamming into him. His expression is piercing, as if he's looking through her, trying to find me inside. I look away, unable to hold his gaze, feeling a mixture of shame and guilt.

"Lie down on the bed," he instructs.

Obeying, I adjust myself into the position I found the body in. When I quit fidgeting, he replaces the pillow on my face.

"Mercy, I need you to take my hand."

The body reaches forward and touches his hand.

"No, Mercy. I need you to leave the body on the bed and take my hand. Concentrate." His voice is firm.

This time the other arm of the body reaches forward. I shove the pillow off of her face and sit up, frustrated. "This isn't working."

I start to think of being stuck this way—in some dead body. Forever. I have to get out.

He sits on the bed next to me."Mercy, take my hand."

Forcing myself to concentrate, I search for his hand and when I find it, I no longer feel cold. Instead, I feel warm, like someone has plugged me back in. The pieces of me are no longer scattered and searching. I feel, for the first time, the separation between the body and myself.

He rearranges the pillow over my face and I sit up. Not the body—me.

As I glance behind me I can see, oddly, that I'm sitting in her. My torso above her, my legs still beneath so I feel for my legs, willing them to slide out. Eventually, they follow and I'm able to rise from the bed.

Expecting the same result as before, I wait for Nathaniel's lack of reaction to my presence in the room, but he stares right at me and says, "That's better."

"You can see me?"

"Yes."

"And hear me?"

That is a stupid question. Obviously, he can hear me because he answered my first question, but still, how is that possible? Why can he see me when Gage can't?

When Nathaniel speaks again it's with such intensity that it takes my breath away. "I've been looking everywhere for you," he says me.

"I'm glad you found me." It's the truth and so I say it. I'm elated that Nathaniel can see me, that around him I feel whole and that when he touches me, I can feel him, really feel him.

He slides his fingers through mine and for a moment we're facing each other.

Nathaniel Black isn't who Gage thinks he is. True, I don't know of all his crimes and I don't want to because it might alter the perception I have of him. Nathaniel's exterior is hard and unyielding. He'll do what he has to do in order to survive and until now I was sure he always put himself first. But he has a way of looking at me, like he'll jump in front of a speeding train to save me.

It's because of that look, the one he's giving me now that tells me that Nathaniel's soul is much deeper than he cares to let on. He is all the things Gage told me about Breachers; he's driven by his desires. But is that really all that bad? Doesn't it also mean that he loves more, cares more?

"Take a walk with me," he says. He takes my hand, leading me out of the house and through the streets to a small park nearby.

He never lets go of my hand and I don't want him to. Feeling connected is exactly what I need. Part of the reason I'm holding onto him is because I fear that if I let go, I'll jump and land in another body. But the other part likes the way my hand fits into his. And I like the way that Nathaniel watches out for me. If I ask him why he's always saving me, I know he'll give me some smartass answer. He isn't going to tell me the truth, and that's okay because I'm not ready to hear it. So I let him hold my hand because, for now, it's what we both need and what we both want.

We pause for a second and I can feel his eagerness to ask me about it, so I tell him. "I didn't kill Lyla."

Nathaniel seems surprised by my answer, but at the same

time he acts like he already knew.

"When I left her body I didn't go anywhere at first. I was in the room with her and then with her and Jay and they couldn't hear me or see me. I thought maybe I was dead." A hiccup catches in my throat as I remember. Nathaniel squeezes my hand.

It gives me the strength to continue. "And then Gage was there and he couldn't hear me or see me at first. But then, I don't know, I wanted him to see me and I made it happen. Only he still couldn't hear me very well. To be on the outside, looking in like that … " I hesitate. "It was awful."

Nathaniel nods as though he understands.

"And then I was gone and it was the strangest sensation. You know how that feels?"

He whispers, "No."

"What do you mean?"

"I'm not like you, Mercy. I'm not attached to this world because I'm not human. And when I Breach, it's because I need a place to go because I can't survive here without a body. But you, you're different."

"Great." I let go of his hand. "I'm a freak among freaks."

Nathaniel places his hands on my shoulders and says, "That's not what I meant." His hands slide down my arms until they find my hands and once again we're linked. "Because you're human, because you have a body all your own, you have roots and your soul is searching for them."

"I don't understand."

"I don't belong here and I have to fight to be here. That's why I Breach. But you belong here. And that's why you can't control the Breaching. You're trying to find your way back."

When he says it like that, it doesn't sound so bad.

"Nathaniel, can I ask you a question?"

"You just did." He laughs. "Ask me anything."

"Why? I mean, I saw the video of you and that nurse ... "
I can't finish.

For the first time since I've known him, a look of shame
alters his facial expression. His eyes narrow and his brow
furrows. "Because I didn't want to die. It really is that simple."

"I have to ask you something else."

"I know you do."

"What did you do? You were a prisoner and you must've
done something, right? I mean they wouldn't punish you like
that for nothing. So, what was it? What did you do?"

He lets go and looks away. "I fell in love."

That is not the answer I expected.

Chapter Thirty-Two

Gage

"**M**ercy! Mercy!" I yell and yell, but she's gone.
Lyla is crying loudly and the sound makes the guilt I already feel double in size. Everywhere I go I bring failure and it's crushing me.

"She's dead." Lyla sobs into Jay's shoulder.

"Is that true?" Jay asks me. "Is Mercy really … ?"

"I'm not sure," I answer honestly.

By all accounts Mercy should be dead. That's what supposed to happen when a soul leaves a body. The soul crosses over to the other side. It's the order of things; the way it's designed. But Breachers break all those laws.

Mercy is different and yet, when her soul lingered, I knew the truth, that she'll never change, that she can't change. But it isn't her fault; it's her nature. It's who she was born to be.

The problem with it all is that I, too, am who I was born to be. I am a Hunter. But the longer I stay among them, the longer

I expose myself to humans and to Breachers, the blurrier the lines get. How can I destroy Mercy? How can I look into her face, her beautiful face, and end her life?

"Gage, what do we do now?" Jay asks, interrupting my thoughts.

Snapping back into solider mode, I make quick decisions. "Go to the hospital and check on your mother. I'll try to find Kate."

"Then I'm coming with you," Lyla says. "I have to find my sister."

"No," Jay and I speak simultaneously.

"I can't protect you and look for your sister at the same time. It's too dangerous," I tell her. "Go to the hospital and wait for me. I'll get there as soon as I can."

There is no more arguing. I escort Lyla and Jay out of the building. When I know they're safe I begin my journey back to the hotel.

A block away from my destination, three black town cars pull up alongside me. The back window of the middle car rolls down. "Get in."

I have no choice but to obey.

The Assembled aren't known to travel outside their realm. They don't enjoy the human world, though they do revel in their power over it. They are the ones who make the rules, who guard the path between life and death. I, as their employee of sorts, have to answer to them.

"Gage," Lucas Church, the eldest of The Assembled, addresses me. "What is the status of your case against Nathaniel Black?"

"Complicated."

The two who sit on either side of Lucas shift in their seats.

On his right is Isadora White and to his left, Donovan Edwards. They frown in disapproval of me.

Isadora leans over and whispers in Lucas's ear. He nods and then addresses me again by saying, "You're dismissed from this case. It has been decided."

"You can't do that!" My reaction is completely out of line and unbecoming of a Hunter.

"We feel as though you can no longer handle this on your own," he continues. "You allowed your team to be killed and your feelings for this Mercy are grounds for penalty."

Isadora fixes her gaze on me. "And my sister? What have you learned of her?"

My hands clench and unclench into fists. "She's alive," I say through gritted teeth.

Isadora, with long legs and dark brown hair that even an industrial strength fan couldn't muss, glares at me with her fierce green eyes. She despises me, that much I can tell. What I don't know is why.

"I need more time," I plead with them.

Isadora gazes out the car window as if she's bored by our conversation. She doesn't even bother to look at me when she says, "You're finished, Gage. Hence forth you are stripped of your Hunter duties. You will serve your sentence out here, among them." Her nose turns up when she says the word *them* as if humans are disgusting creatures.

"You have no authority!"

Her head snaps around and she snarls at me when she says, "I have all the authority. That you've forgotten only proves my point. You are worthless to us. You sympathize with them. You love one of them. So now, you will be one of them."

The third Assembled, the quiet one, clenches my wrist.

Twice my size, with muscles that his black suit barely contains, he squeezes and I buckle, crying out in pain. Pulling back my shirtsleeve, he exposes my mark, my Hunter's mark. It's a tattoo of sorts, but more of a brand. From his pocket he removes a gold knife and with ease, like I am nothing more than a loaf of bread, he slices the brand off of my arm.

When they're finished, I am thrown from the car and forced to watch them drive off. Blood drips from my forearm to the concrete. Before I bleed out, I take off my shirt and wind it around my wrist.

The pain and blood are only minor distractions that last momentarily. It isn't long before I'm once again dealing with the real issues. I am no longer a Hunter.

I have no purpose, no direction, no focus, and no plan. Is this what it's like to be cast out? Being that I always believed Nathaniel was in the wrong, I never thought of the consequences he suffered.

Come to think of it, I never even questioned the severity of his crimes. It wasn't my place to question The Assembled. But now, now all I can do was question everything because I have nothing.

My decision-making skills are completely out of whack, so I can't say that I was thinking clearly when I decided that charging into the hotel was going to be my next move.

* * *

A few people in the lobby gawk at my bloody arm and one even offers to help, but I brush him off and beeline to the elevators.

I have no idea what Ariana's reaction will be. There's a good chance she'll kill me on sight. Part of me wishes she will.

With my good arm, I bang on the door. "Ariana!" The door next to hers opens and a silver-haired man pokes his head into the hall.

"Get back inside." He quickly responds to my request.

"Ariana!" I yell again. "Let me in!"

The lock clicks and the door opens just a crack. "What's your purpose here?" one of her lackeys asks me.

Kicking the door with all of my strength, it flies open and knocks the unsuspecting man backward into the room. He springs to his feet, but not before I draw my weapon. He continues to back away slowly.

The room is like any other penthouse suite, ornately decorated to the point of being gaudy. Two other men, who sit poised and ready to pounce, occupy the sitting area. They eye my wound. They know they'll be able to overtake me and so I yell again, "Ariana!"

The double doors to the bedroom area are off to the right. When they open, Ariana steps out in all her glory. Her auburn hair is ironed straight, hanging in sheets next to her face. Her green eyes practically glow while her lips form the faintest smile.

"Gage, to what do I owe the pleasure?" She saunters across the room to the bar cart, uncaps a bottle of whiskey and pours herself a glass. Though she offers me one, I wave her off, gun still in my hand.

"Have a seat," she says politely.

Cautiously, I follow her to the sitting area. The two men move, allowing us to sit. They lurk behind Ariana, flanking her, arms crossed in a protective stance.

"We need to talk alone," I tell her and nod to her bodyguards.

"I'll lower mine, if you lower yours." She motions to my gun.

Slowly, I place it on the table as a sign of good faith. She and I both know I have other weapons and that this is only a gesture, but she seems willing enough to play along.

With a slight flick of her head, she instructs her bodyguards to leave us, which they do. If she needs them, they aren't far. She's completely confident in her ability to overtake me.

Sipping her whiskey, she crosses her legs and leans back into the couch. Showing me that she's perfectly comfortable is another power play. I lean forward showing her that I am not intimidated.

"You're bleeding," she points out.

Gingerly as possible, I raise my sleeve and expose the gash in my skin. Though she tries to hide it, her entire body freezes. To cover, she slowly sips her drink.

"Ethan!" she yells. Almost instantly one of the body guards returns. "Get Gage some rags and a bandage before he ruins the carpet."

Ethan fetches the items. When I press the warm rag to my skin, I grimace.

"Let me," Ariana offers. She sits next to me on the couch and with the care of a mother, she cleans and dresses my wound.

"Thank you."

"You have questions." She leaves my side and sits across from me. "You aren't the only one."

"What do you want to know?" I ask her.

"Where is my daughter?"

"I don't know."

Again, her body tenses. Her lips set into a thin line and

she does not blink. When she does move again, it's slow, purposeful. She refills her glass at the bar cart and this time, she doesn't ask if I want a drink, but she hands me one anyway.

I take a small sip and let the liquid burn down my throat and into my gut. Quickly, the burning morphs to warming and I feel myself settle in a bit.

"I thought you were keeping Mercy at the meat packing plant. But she wasn't there."

"Keeping Mercy hostage in a meat-packing plant? No, my dear boy, that wasn't me."

There's innuendo in her statement as well as accusation. "But I thought ... "

She interrupts, "You thought wrong."

"Why did you come here?"

She laughs. "What do you know about Guides, Gage?"

"Guides?"

"Yes. That's what I was before I became ... " she pauses " ... this."

"Guides are the ones who help the souls cross over. They find the lost, the ones that remain and they help them."

"Exactly."

"What does this have to do with anything?"

"You've been fighting this war your entire life. Wouldn't you like to at least know why?"

Ariana readjusts herself on the couch, like she wants to get comfortable before telling me her story. No matter how cooperative she's being, it's never far from my mind that we're enemies.

"Guides, like me," she begins, "were governed by The Assembled. The rules were simple. Do your job, ask no questions, follow orders, don't break the rules."

"What rules?"

"Same as yours; no human interaction." She shrugs. "Seems simple enough and yet, over time, things got ... " she takes a healthy swig of her drink before adding, " ... complicated."

Impatient, I wait for her to go on. She enjoys having the power over me, enjoys that I'm at her mercy.

"Humans have such freedom, such luxury to live as they please. As you know, we are not afforded the same. We are slaves."

I flinch at the word slave. I never saw it that way. We have extremely important positions, which require a sense of duty that most beings, especially humans, can't provide.

"To put it simply," Ariana says, "I wanted more."

"You wanted more?"

"Yes, I wanted more. I wanted what they had, choices, experiences."

"Why didn't you just ask to leave?"

Ariana laughs deeply. "You think I didn't?" She's mocking me.

I am beginning to understand. "They didn't let you. The Assembled, I mean, they refused."

"Of course they refused! They needed me to do their dirty work."

"I don't understand."

"Who crosses over, who doesn't, they decide. And the ones that are left are ... " She doesn't finish her sentence, instead taking another drink.

"What?"

"Discarded."

The very idea sickens me. Why would The Assembled do that?

"It was Nathaniel who broke the laws first. He was supposed to help her cross over. He loved her and so I helped him and together, we became outlaws."

"You were sentenced to be human. You got what you wanted."

"What we *wanted*?" She rises from the couch and towers over me. "This is not what we wanted! We've been discarded, Gage. Just like you."

What she said doesn't make sense. They interfered in human life and so they were given the chance to be human. And at the end of that life, they should've crossed over. But they didn't.

I've always thought it was their choice. But what if it wasn't? What if the true punishment was becoming a Breacher? It couldn't be, and yet …

"I don't understand," I tell her.

She slams the glass down on the table. "Let me spell it out. The Assembled tricked us. They didn't make us human. We just became a different type of slave. They wanted to use us to manipulate the humans, to tilt the world and put it on its knees. We breached the bodies they wanted and we thought, maybe, if we continued to do their work that they'd give us what we'd asked for, our own lives. But they never did. Century after century we started wars, ended lives, did whatever they asked. And when we finally refused, well, that's when you came along."

Chapter Thirty-Three

Mercy

Nathaniel is quiet. I don't want to pry, but I want to hear the rest of his story. I try to picture him in love, being tender or sweet with a woman. It isn't that difficult to imagine. Nathaniel is driven and downright scary at times, but he's showing me the real side of him, the caring side.

When the silence is too much for me I ask him. "Will you tell me about her?"

He looks into my eyes and says, "It doesn't matter. She's gone."

There's such pain behind his words and I want nothing more than to take it all away. It's important to me that he trust me, that he know I'm not going to do anything to betray him. The war between him and Gage is just that—their war. As far as I'm concerned, I am Switzerland.

"You can tell me," I tell him.

He exhales. "Her name was Ellie. She was young and

beautiful with hair that I wanted to tangle myself in forever."

It's difficult to listen to him describe his love for someone else, more difficult than I expected.

"But I wasn't allowed to know her," he continues. "It was forbidden for me, as her Guide."

"Her Guide?"

"When you die," he tells me, "a Guide is there to help you cross to the other side."

"So, what happened?"

"I revealed myself to her, which is entirely forbidden. Every night, I'd go to her and talk to her about what it would be like to be on the other side. She wouldn't be sick. She wouldn't be scared."

Nathaniel clears his throat. "She didn't have much time left. All I wanted was to be with her." He exhales slowly. "When I was sentenced, I thought I'd live one lifetime and die. That's what we were told. But that wasn't what happened. We were used, Mercy. Breachers were used as puppets and we did the bidding of The Assembled. I've done terrible things. Things you can't even imagine. When I tried to escape, they ripped a rib from my body and created my brother and forced him to hunt me down."

He releases me and steps back, raking his fingers through his dark hair. It's nearly impossible for his eyes to get any blacker and yet they do. The fury he feels turns them midnight on a starless night.

When he looks like that I fear him, but I know that he won't hurt me and so it isn't so much of a choice as it is a gut reaction to go to him. My right hand finds its way to the side of his face and though he resists at first, he eventually settles into my gaze.

We study each other's faces as his hands explore my arms, working their way around to the back of my neck. He curls my hair around his fingers and lets it drop. The sensation when he touches me exhilarates and ignites my skin, which is odd, because I'm not wearing my skin.

I almost laugh when I realize that if someone were to walk by, they will only see Nathaniel and that will appear odd, to say the least.

But it doesn't matter to me if anyone walks by and sees what's happening. Everything I want is right in front of me. Nathaniel looks at me so intensely that it isn't long before the world disappears and all that exists are he and I.

I flinch when he leans closer, not because I don't want him to do what he's about to do, but because I want the moment before to last longer. He seems to understand me. When he leans in again, he lingers.

His lips hover above mine, our breath mingles together and then neither of us can take it any longer, though he has more control than I. He brushes his lips to mine, gently, with caution as if he's waiting for my answer to his advance.

I inch closer to him, pressing myself against him as I shape my mouth to his. We work in rhythm, give and take, push and pull.

I could have kissed him forever. That's why when he pulls away and whispers, "Mercy, I can't do this," my heart nearly fractures in two.

Chapter Thirty-Four

Gage

It can't be true. All the things Ariana is saying, they can't possibly be true. The Assembled are not the monsters she's making them out to be. She's twisting this around so that I'll feel sorry for her. Her powers of manipulation are like nothing I've ever experienced before. She almost has me convinced, but luckily, I catch myself before I fall too deep into her web of lies.

Ariana is a Breacher. She steals other people's bodies so that she can continue to live. The Assembled have nothing to do with it. They created me to end Breachers. What she is accusing them of isn't possible.

There's one small thing that's nagging me and though I know I will regret asking, I can't help myself.

"How are you alive?"

"That's a curious thing, Gage, considering you killed me."

The battle between Ariana and I took place on Mercy's tenth birthday. They'd gone to San Francisco for the day and I'd followed them. They spent their time shopping and enjoying each other's company. They looked happy.

Ariana dropped Mercy off at school near the end of the day. That's when I knew she was on to me. She made sure Mercy was safe first.

Taking her out was easy, almost too easy. Rae and I approached the house and Ariana was on the porch sipping tea. She didn't put up much of a fight when I attacked.

We didn't just discard her, we separated her into pieces and scattered them across the beyond. For her to be sitting here in front of me there has to be an act of, well, an act of The Assembled.

"I don't believe it," I tell her.

"Whether you believe it or not doesn't make it any less true. The Assembled brought me back. They needed me to do their work. They still do. But I'm done playing it their way."

"What does that mean?"

"It means, Gage, that I'm going to kill them. I'm going to kill every single one of them and if you stand in my way, I won't even blink before killing you as well."

"And Mercy? What are your plans for her?"

Ariana's wicked smile spreads across her face. "I'm sure you've pieced it together by now that Mercy isn't an ordinary Breacher. She has a special gift that makes her uniquely qualified to assist me."

"Mercy isn't interested in fighting your battles, Ariana."

One step too far. She sneers at me. "You know nothing of my daughter, Gage. And thanks to you, she knows nothing of me. But things change."

"I won't let you get away with this!"

"You think you know what's going on, but you don't. The mere fact that you think I'd lock my daughter in some meat packing plant is evidence enough. You want to know who burned down your warehouse, who killed your precious team? Go ask The Assembled."

My mouth cracks open. I stare at her in disbelief as I replay her words in my head. "No. They wouldn't." I shake my head.

"Open your eyes! The truth is right in front of you."

Ariana heads back toward the bedroom. As she approaches the doors she spins around and calls, "Ethan!"

The bodyguard returns, all hulking six-foot-three of him.

"Show Gage to the door."

He steps toward me and I'm off the couch in one quick motion. "Don't do this, Ariana. Don't drag Mercy into all of this."

She seems to consider my request.

"I can see that you have feelings for her, which you and I both know is the reason why you were cast out. You are of no use to The Assembled, but you can be of use to me. We're on the same side. Mercy's side. I will do whatever I have to do to protect her and I will destroy whomever stands in my way. That's your choice, Gage: Help me protect Mercy, or be destroyed by the lies The Assembled fed you."

* * *

As I walk the streets of midtown, I feel clueless, lost, broken. Moisture fills the corners of my eyes and slowly trickles down my face. I swipe the tears away as quickly as I can. Hunters are above petty emotions, but I am no longer a Hunter. I am human. And my whole life is a lie.

If this is what it means to be human, to succumb to feelings, to feel destroyed, then I'd rather pass.

I wander until I end up in a small park. Across the way, I see the strangest sight. A man is kissing someone, but there's no one there. It's like he's kissing the air. As I draw closer I realize what I'm seeing. My gut twists into knots.

Nathaniel is kissing Mercy.

I have this overwhelming urge to beat him senseless.

"Nathaniel!" I call to him and jog over.

He doesn't exactly look thrilled to see me.

"Mercy is with you." There's no point in dancing around; he can't deny what I just saw. She's there with him and they were just kissing.

"She breached the body of a dead girl, so getting her out was, well, let's call it messy. What happened on your end?"

Rolling up my shirtsleeve, I expose my wrist. "Had a little chat with The Assembled."

He raises an eyebrow at me. "Cast you out, did they?"

"Yes. And I've seen Ariana. She told me everything."

Nathaniel laughs and rubs his chin. "Did she?"

"Why didn't you tell me?"

"You say that like you would've believed me. You were created to destroy me, remember?"

He has a point, but that does nothing to lessen my anger.

Nathaniel asks, "What exactly did she tell you?"

"Her version of the truth."

"You've had your whole world turned upside down. I know how that feels. But I'm not willing to give up and you can't either. We can fix this."

"Ariana wants to fight The Assembled. She told me she's going to kill them all."

Chapter Thirty-Five

Mercy

Everything is shifting. Seeing Gage fall apart is startling. But I understand what he's going through. His whole world has been upended and he has to reconcile that. Nothing is black and white anymore. What he believed is a sham. It must be hell for him to face it all.

It's hell for me also. Just a few days ago, I considered myself fairly average, and fairly lucky to have a calm life. I didn't know that my entire life has been a lie as well. Nothing about me is ordinary or usual. I've faced horror after horror. The dead bodies are piling up around me.

When I touch Gage, I can really feel him. I know he can feel me when his hand slides over mine.

"I'm sorry," he whispers to me.

"I know."

"This is all so much. I can't … "

"You can't breathe. I get it."

He holds onto me. I feel whole, nearly the same way I do when Nathaniel touches me. Behind me, I feel Nathaniel tense up in reaction to Gage and I being so close.

I have no idea how to fix any of this. As I stand there, knee deep in self-pity, I think of Lyla. She breaks me out of my head.

"Gage, are Lyla and Jay safe?"

Gage's whole demeanor changes when I mention their names. The soldier in him is always just below the surface. He reaches for it so easily. "I sent them to the hospital to check on Jay's mother."

"And Kate? Did you find her?"

"No. She wasn't at the warehouse and I don't think Ariana has her either."

"What makes you say that?" Nathaniel asks him.

"If Ariana had Kate she would've used her as leverage, but she didn't."

It isn't easy to hear Gage speak of my mother in such a way. Though I know that, like Nathaniel, my mother has blood on her hands, I'm holding onto the hope that she won't do anything to harm the people I love.

"We need to find Kate," I tell them both. "Lyla must be going crazy by now."

"Mercy, there's not much you can do in your condition," Gage says to me.

"Actually, Mercy is quite useful this way. She can slip around unnoticed," Nathaniel tells him.

"What if she breaches again? It's too risky. She has no control," Gage points out.

"I won't let that happen," Nathaniel says forcefully.

But Gage is not deterred. "How? By kissing her again?"

"If that's what it takes." Nathaniel's lips pull up into a wicked grin.

Gage looks as though he could throttle Nathaniel. I step in and end this ridiculous discussion.

"Stop! Gage is right, Nathaniel. I don't have a hold here. And I don't want to breach any more bodies. I need to get back into mine."

"But we have a better chance against The Assembled if you stay like this. They'll never see you coming," Nathaniel protests.

"You're putting too much faith in me, Nathaniel. And if we're not careful I could end up halfway around the world. And then what would you do?"

"I will find you wherever you are," Nathaniel professes.

His assertion of feelings toward me makes me blush. Gage avoids eye contact with me.

"Go with Gage to the hospital," I tell Nathaniel. "See if Kate is there, please."

Gage's brow furrows as a suspicious look contorts his face. "What are you going to do?" he asks me.

Taking a deep breath and exhaling slowly, I look at both of them when I say, "I'm going to see Ariana."

I can see that both Gage and Nathaniel are about to protest. I don't give them the chance.

"Please do this for me," I ask them both. "I'll be fine, I promise."

Reluctantly, they agree, but they insist on escorting me to the hotel. It isn't difficult for me to agree to this, especially after they remind me that The Assembled are out there somewhere looking for me.

We part ways at the elevator doors. The elevator rides

all the way to the penthouse without stopping. For that I am grateful. Even though I know that no one can see me or hear me, I feel safer by myself. Gage is absolutely right that I have no control over my breaching.

About two feet from my mother's hotel room door, I freeze. The surge of bravery I felt in the park dissipates and reality sets in. For the first time in six years, I am about to come face to face with my mother.

As I close in on the hotel room, every inch of me begins to vibrate with fear. It's not just that I'm about to see my mother again. Something about the whole scene feels wrong. The door is slightly ajar. This alone should've told me to run, but like an idiot girl in a slasher movie, I press on. I've come this far and I can't just turn around and leave because I'm scared.

Carefully, I toe the door open with the front of my shoe and step inside. The room is in shambles. Tables are toppled, drapes torn, couches overturned; it's clear that a fight has taken place.

Just beyond the first couch a shoe pokes out. Edging closer I see a rather large man lying on the floor face down. His face is smashed in and blood leaks out of his ears, his mouth, and what's left of his nose. The entire sight turns my stomach and I have to avert my eyes.

Beyond the main room there are double doors, which I assume lead to a bedroom. They're wide open and the bedroom is in the same condition as the main room. It's a disaster. Another body is on the floor with much the same look as the first one.

Next to the bed are medical supplies, monitors, and IV stands with half-used bags of fluid hanging from them. If my body had been here, it's long gone now. I'm beginning to think that I will never find my body.

To the left of the bed there's blood splatter all across the walls. Only there isn't a body. My mother is nowhere in sight. If this blood is hers, she isn't in good shape.

I hear a noise coming from the living room. Quickly I duck to hide behind the doors. The intruder is a woman with sharp features and the slickest ponytail I've ever seen. Though I know I should be very worried for my safety, I can't help thinking that Lyla would be seriously impressed with this lady's fashion skills.

She inspects the room, careful not to actually touch anything or step in any blood. When she's done, she turns in my direction.

"Hello, Mercy."

Feeling sheepish, I stand.

"I'm your Aunt Isadora."

I have an aunt? Could this possibly get any weirder? "Where's my mother?"

"Dead, I hope."

It's impossible to hide my shock. "What?"

"She's a criminal. She may have escaped our custody until now, but that is no longer the case. And when the interrogation is over, she'll be disposed of, as she should have years ago."

There's no hint of remorse or compassion in her tone. She speaks of my mother as if she's trash, easily discarded and forgotten about.

"You're one of the Assembled?"

She smiles, but not in a friendly way. "I see Gage and Nathaniel have brought you up to speed."

There's no way I am going to give her any information. "I know enough."

"You know nothing," she replies.

Her green eyes are the same color as my mothers, but there's no light behind them, no love. They are full of hate and spite. "You're going to come with me."

It is not a request.

Cursing myself for coming alone, I know I have two options, go with her or fight. Or maybe there's a third option, if I'm stupid enough to try it.

Without knowing where I'll end up or in whom, breaching seems like a ridiculous idea, but it might get me back to Nathaniel. He found me the last time, so there's a chance that he'll find me again.

But what if he doesn't? And what if I can't find a way to get out without killing the body? What if I only got lucky when it came to Lyla? There are so many reasons not to do what I'm about to do.

Both Nathaniel and Gage warned me about a Breachers instinct to survive. They explained that it's a compulsion more than a virtue. They are right because what I feel inside me is a need so strong that it's not to be ignored. Going with Isadora will lead to my death in one way or another, of that I'm sure and therefore, it isn't an option.

There's a chance I'll win in a fight, but there's a chance I'll lose also. The only guarantee of my safety is to breach.

Lord, help me.

Chapter Thirty-Six

Gage

The hospital is much more crowded than it had been earlier so it's easier to slip by unnoticed. Nathaniel and I do a quick check around and don't find anything to be out of the ordinary.

We find Lyla, Jay, and Mercy's father in the cafeteria. When Lyla spots me she jumps up and comes running.

"Did you find Mercy?"

Unsure of what to say to her, I pause for a second too long.

"Something's wrong. I can tell. What is it?"

Lyla's blue eyes are like crystals, hard and mesmerizing. Her dark hair frames her face in such a way that makes them practically pop from her face. Lyla is stunningly beautiful and I can only imagine how she uses her beauty to her advantage. It would be difficult to say no to a face like hers.

Studying her in such a way is odd for me, mostly because I've never taken the time to consider a human before I saw Mercy. They were sort of faceless to me before, more like dots on a map, but now, I'm really beginning to see the world around me.

Not only am I seeing everything as if it were new, I am feeling them too. From Lyla's expression I know that she's concerned, but it isn't just by her look, it's the way she hunches forward, the way her shoulders are raised to her ears. Hope and worry emanate from her as she projects her feelings outward.

"Mercy is all right." As far as I know. "She went to see her mother."

"Her mother!" Lyla shakes her head. "I may never get used to that." She turns her attention to Nathaniel. "Who are you?"

Nathaniel and I exchange a look. It's better to keep things simple. "This is … "

"I'm his brother," Nathaniel interrupts.

Lyla seems satisfied with this answer. "What do we do now?"

I have absolutely no idea what to do, so I change the subject. "How's Jay's mom?"

"Mrs. Sheller is going to be fine, but she'll have to stay in the hospital for a few days. *Kate* went home to get her things," Lyla answers.

Kate! I'd almost forgotten that we were looking for her.

"So Kate wasn't missing like we'd thought," Nathaniel says.

"The battery in her cell died and she hadn't checked it for messages."

Nathaniel elbows me. "This is good news."

"Right. Very good news," I agree. Knowing Kate is safe will make Mercy happy.

By now Jay and Mercy's father are watching us. We make our way over to the table and introductions are made.

"Gage," Mr. Clare shakes my hand. "You were with my Mercy when ... " He trails off, unable to finish.

"I'm sorry that I didn't talk to you sooner," I tell him. It surprises me that I mean it.

It appears as though the Hunter method of handling things may not have been the most considerate way, which is why I take this opportunity to say to Jay, "I'm very sorry about your mother."

"The police think it was a robbery," Jay informs me.

Mr. Clare lets out the faintest of snorts. Lyla and Jay don't notice anything, but Nathaniel and I both notice. Mr. Clare doesn't think it was a robbery, which makes me wonder about Mr. Clare and what exactly he knows about his wife's breaching.

"I'm glad she's going to be okay," I say. "My brother and I were concerned."

"Deeply," Nathaniel says with too much sarcasm.

Jay glares at Nathaniel and I think for a moment that Jay might lash out, but instead he breathes deeply and says, "I'm going to go check on my mom."

"I'll come with you," Lyla offers.

Alone at the table with Mercy's father, an uncomfortable and awkward silence fills the air.

Nathaniel leans across the table and says, "So, Eric, why don't you tell us all you know about Ariana and Breachers."

My head whips in his direction and I want to throttle him for being so tactless, but then I notice how Mercy's father doesn't even flinch.

"You know something," I say to him.

Eric Clare slides deeper into the chair and folds his arms. He lets out a deep sigh.

"Look, we can do this the easy way," Nathaniel begins, "or

we can do this the fun way."

I give Nathaniel a reproachful glare, then turn my attention back to Eric. "If you know something, you're in danger. We can help you."

Eric snorts. "Like you helped my little girl?"

I didn't see that coming. By the way Nathaniel tenses, I know that he didn't either.

"We are trying to help her," I tell him.

Eric's eyes narrow. "You are the reason this happened. Mercy was safe until you came along."

Nathaniel's jaw tightens and he looks like he could rage, but he keeps his composure.

"Mr. Clare, sir, Mercy and Ariana are together now," I tell him. "Soon, Mercy will be back in her body and then everything will be right again."

"The Assembled won't let that happen. And you know it."

Nathaniel and I look at each other. We both understand then that Mercy's father knows everything. How or when Ariana told him the truth—that doesn't matter now. What matters is that he knows. And that means he's in jeopardy.

"I don't understand," Nathaniel begins. "If you knew, why didn't you tell Mercy? Why did you leave her so vulnerable?"

Eric wipes his hand across his mouth. "There was no way to know if Mercy was a Breacher. So we hoped. *I* hoped. All I wanted was a normal life for my little girl. I didn't want any of this for her."

"I was trying to help her," Nathaniel explains to him.

Anger seethes from Eric as he speaks. "Why do you think Ariana faked her death? Because she knew that her mere presence around Mercy might trigger this. But *you*? You just couldn't stay away."

As long as we are laying our cards on the table, I decide to correct him. "Ariana didn't fake her death. I killed her."

Eric shakes his head. "She let you kill her so that The Assembled would leave Mercy alone. With Ariana out of the picture, Mercy and I were free to try and live a normal life. We sacrificed everything to give Mercy a chance."

Nathaniel hangs his head as he realizes what Eric is saying. Mercy was safe this whole time. The Assembled didn't know what she was and so they weren't hunting her. They brought Ariana back from the dead and used her. She went along with it to keep them away from Mercy. If Nathaniel hadn't stepped in, none of this would've happened. And if I'd done my job, if I'd killed Nathaniel like I was supposed to, he wouldn't have been around to find Mercy.

All along we were both trying to protect Mercy. But we'd done the exact opposite.

Nathaniel shoves back from the table and storms off. There will be time to chase him down, but for now I am unable to move.

"He didn't," I start. "I mean, we didn't … We never meant for any of this to happen."

"Please find my daughter and my wife before The Assembled do."

He leaves me sitting there. Alone with my guilt, with my grief, I hold my head in my hands and squeeze, hoping it will stop the incessant pounding. How did everything get so out of hand?

This is all my fault. I'm the one who ultimately put Mercy in jeopardy. The guilt is relentless.

But maybe it isn't too late to fix it. If Mercy and Ariana are together, they're a force to be reckoned with. It's possible they can take down The Assembled and set things right again. I need to get back to the hotel.

* * *

Nathaniel is there as I step off the elevator. It doesn't surprise me that he's on the same path.

"Something happened," he tells me.

"What? What is it?" I try to move past him, but he holds me back. "Is it Mercy? Tell me!"

"I don't know! There's blood everywhere. Ariana's goons are dead. There's no body, no Ariana, no Mercy."

"Son of a bitch!" I kick the wall as hard as I can.

Nathaniel grasps me by the shoulders and shakes me. "Gage! Look at me!" Reluctantly I obey. "We don't know the worst has happened, so let's focus and come up with a plan."

He's right. We need a plan. But nothing I can think of sounds even remotely possible. All roads lead to taking on The Assembled. Nathaniel knows it and so do I. The question is how.

"It'll never work," I say. "We're not strong enough."

"We're not, but Mercy is."

"What are you talking about?"

There's conviction in his tone. "Think about it, Gage. Why else would they want her so badly? This isn't about you, or me, or even Ariana. This is about Mercy. They fear her, which means—well, I don't know exactly what it means, but we need to find out."

Hearing Nathaniel say it, I have to admit there's something

to his theory. Why else would The Assembled step in now? They knew where Ariana is and they knew Nathaniel is alive and yet they only made an appearance when Mercy became involved.

This means that there's a very strong possibility that they haven't killed her. If she has skills they think they can use, they'll certainly try to manipulate her until they get their way. Just like they'd used me, they'll use her. The question is, what for? What do they want from her?

"Where would they have taken her?" Nathaniel asks.

"I don't know."

"Think."

Taking a moment to consider, an idea strikes me. "They would've taken her to the warehouse, but Ariana's men destroyed it."

"Is your warehouse the only one?"

"What do you mean?"

"I mean, little brother, with your team out of the way, The Assembled would've created more Hunters, which means they would've built a new warehouse."

"It's possible, I guess."

It's more than possible. That's exactly the kind of thing they would do. But that isn't what worries me. What worries me is how The Assembled will make new Hunters. If I was created from Nathaniel, that means that to stop Mercy, they'll need to make a Hunter from her.

"They wouldn't."

"You're not so sure about that are you?"

I'm not. The idea that The Assembled might pull from Mercy to create new Hunters sickens me. But Nathaniel has a point; it's their M.O. We have to find their new warehouse and fast.

Chapter Thirty-Seven

Mercy

There isn't time for Isadora to stop me. I'm not even sure she realizes what I'm about to do before it's too late. This time, when I jump, I feel like I splinter. I'm afraid that I won't be able to put myself back together again. It's difficult, but I manage to channel my energy in one direction. I still feel like I'm in pieces, but I have control over the swarm.

When I land, all the air escapes my lungs and I'm struck with the sudden urge to vomit. Checking myself over, I can see that I am exactly where I wanted to go, whom I wanted to be in: Kate.

I couldn't take Lyla's body again; I'd already put her through enough. And I couldn't take Jay's because I didn't want to be in the body of a guy. That would be weird.

So I chose Kate because she's close to home and she's familiar. There's a twinge of guilt that comes along with this breach, but my self-preservation wins out in the end. Kate is at

Jay's house when I breach her. She looks to be in the middle of gathering Mrs. Sheller's things. Once the nausea and spinning subside, I stretch out into her skin and finish her task. I'm about to head back to the hospital when I encounter a snag.

I don't know how to drive. Walking to the hospital will take forever so there's really only one option. The keys are in Kate's pocket. The car is in the drive. I could kick myself for telling my dad that I wasn't interested in learning to drive. Then I say a silent prayer that I don't kill us both.

Sliding into the driver's seat, I put the keys in the ignition and turn it over. As soon as the engine is purring, I hear a voice, Kate's voice, in my head. She knows exactly what to do and she guides me along. Using my left foot I release the emergency break and with my right hand I shift the gear into reverse. I hit the brakes suddenly more than once, but I manage to back the car out of the drive.

Driving to the hospital is tricky to say the least, but every time I start to panic, I hear Kate's voice telling me what to do. Soon, I'm pulling into a space in the hospital parking lot. After so many setbacks, it feels amazing to accomplish something, even if it is just driving.

I run straight to the information desk and inquire about Mrs. Sheller. The helpful volunteer gives me the room number. Jay and Lyla are at Mrs. Sheller's bedside when I arrive.

"How is she?" I ask.

"The same, stable," Jay answers.

Setting the bag on the floor, I move to stand next to Jay. "I'm glad she's going to be okay, Jay."

"Thanks," he says.

Turning to Lyla I say, "Ly, would you grab me a cup of coffee?"

"I'm not your servant, Kate."

"Seriously? You can't even do me a small favor?"

"Fine, I'll be right back."

With Lyla out of the room I take the opportunity to talk to Jay. "I have to tell you something," I start. "And you're not going to like it. But more importantly, no matter what, you cannot tell Lyla what I've done."

"Holy shit! Mercy?"

"How did you know?"

"It's the way you stand. Your left foot is turned in, that's classic you."

Looking down I see that Jay is right. My left foot is slightly turned in. "Oh." I correct my stance.

Jay backs away from me. "What have you done?"

He's disgusted by me. It's written all over his face.

"Jay, I had to. They were going to take me."

"So you took Kate? Mercy, this isn't right, you can't keep taking other people's bodies."

It infuriates me that he's judging me and not giving me a chance to explain. "There isn't time to make you understand why I did what I did. I need to find Gage and Nathaniel. Do you know where they are?"

He shakes his head. "They're looking for you, I think. They could be anywhere."

"And you have no clue? That's helpful."

Jay is more than offended by my sarcastic tone. "What's with you? This isn't you. This thing you're becoming. It's not you."

"This is the new me. You'll get over it."

We're both stunned by my words. Jay backs away even farther until he's flattened against the wall.

"I'm sorry. I didn't mean it. There's this part of me that keeps coming forward and I can't fight it."

"I don't know what's happening to you, Mercy. I'm your friend, your best friend, so I'm trying to understand. Bur first, you took my girlfriend and then my mom nearly got killed, so my patience for this whole situation is running out at this point."

"I'm not trying to hurt any of you."

"I get that. I do. But it's difficult to understand when you're standing here in Kate's body. Your life may have been in danger, or whatever, but that doesn't give you the right to take hers."

"Are you blaming me? Because this isn't my fault. This is happening to me too. I didn't ask for this."

"I'm not blaming you, Mercy."

"Well, it sounds like you are."

I need to take a deep breath before the anger takes over completely. Fighting with Jay is not productive. He's scared and frustrated and maybe even right that I shouldn't have taken Kate's body. Arguing with Jay is wasting time and I need to find Gage and Nathaniel.

"Jay, I'm really sorry. And I'll fix this, I promise, but right now I have to go."

Lyla returns and she senses right away that there's tension between us. She looks at both of us accusingly, knowingly. "What's going on?"

Silently, I plead with Jay to keep my secret. By the way he glares at me I can tell that he's in the throes of a dilemma. He doesn't want to help me by lying to Lyla, but he doesn't want to upset her either.

Finally he says, "Nothing. Everything's fine."

Thank you, I mouth to him. To Lyla I say, "Thanks for the coffee. I'm going to go check on my ... um, Eric. I'm going to go check on Eric."

As quickly as I can, I duck out of the room and head back to the waiting room. My dad is sitting in a chair with his head tilted back against the wall. His eyes are closed, but I know he's not sleeping.

"Eric?"

"Is something wrong? Is Sharon okay?" He's asking about Jay's mother.

"She's fine," I assure him. "I just wanted to tell you that I'm sorry about the mix up with Mercy. But I'm sure everything's going to be fine soon."

His expression changes. His eyes narrow and he leans closer. "Is that you, Ariana?"

All the wind sucks out of my lungs and I feel that my legs might give way at any moment. He knows! He knows? He knows about my mother. But that's no guarantee that he knows about me as well.

Slowly, I shake my head. A small tear worms its way to the corner of my eye and hesitates only momentarily before careening down my cheek.

"Mercy?"

The single tear has company and it isn't long before streams of moisture drench my face. My dad envelops me up in a hug that I hope will last forever. I'm no longer alone. The fear that he might hate me, or that he won't accept me if he ever finds out what I am, is gone.

"Daddy," I whisper. "I'm so sorry."

"Oh honey, I'm so happy you're safe. I thought for sure those idiots were going to get you killed."

Pulling back, I wipe my face and dab at the wet stain on his shirt. "What do you mean?"

"Gage and Nathaniel. They're the reason you're in this mess."

My mind begins to reel. It's one thing for my dad to know about me, but this is almost too much. And he has it wrong. Gage and Nathaniel are trying to help me. True, Gage has lied to me along the way, but I know, at the heart of it, he's only trying to protect me.

"No," I explain. "It's not their fault."

"Mercy, listen to me. You have to stay away from them. They're going to get you killed." He looks around to make sure no one is listening. "Your mother is at the Sheraton Grand, the penthouse suite. Go to her. She'll help you."

Oh God. What am I supposed to tell him now?

I have to tell him the truth. He deserves to know that there's a chance, a real chance this time, that his wife, my mother is dead.

"I have to tell you something," I begin. "I've already been to the hotel."

The look of hope that spreads across his face is so touching and it breaks my heart to know that I'm about to dash it.

"You've seen her?"

"No," I answer quietly. "She wasn't there. But Isadora was."

I don't need to say more because he seems to understand what I'm implying, but I need to tell him everything. "She told me The Assembled took Mom and that once they were done questioning her … " Try as I might, I can't finish the sentence.

"They're lying. They won't kill her. Not until they have you."

"How do you know that?"

My dad rubs the back of his neck. "I just know, but not all the details. Your mother didn't want me to know everything, she said it was better, safer for me if I didn't."

I already know what he doesn't. I'm not the average Breacher. If I was, I would've killed Lyla. This is the bottom line. It all boils down to me. The reason Gage's friends were killed, the reason Jay's mother was attacked, the reason my mother was being held hostage; it's all because of me. Unlike what I told Jay earlier, this wasn't happening *to* me; it was happening *because* of me.

That means that it's up to me to stop it all. It's in my hands to be able to save everyone.

"I have to go," I say to him. "But first, I need you to do something for me."

"Anything."

"Help Kate."

He understands what I mean and so he waits.

Before I leave Kate's body, I have to say, in case it's my last opportunity, "I love you, Daddy."

"I love you too, baby girl."

We hug once more and he holds my face in his hands. I don't want to let go, but I know I have to, so I close my eyes and try to break myself free. There isn't any pain this time, only the agony of letting go of my dad.

He holds Kate's body when she slumps over. I don't know what he'll tell her when she wakes, but I know he'll cover for me.

In truth, I much prefer being in a body, even if it isn't my own. When this first happened and I found myself in Lyla's body, there was nothing I wanted more than to claw my way out. The dead body I breached was even worse. There is nothing creepier than that.

But being without a body at all is awful. On the outside looking in, unable to touch or communicate is torture. Of course, even without a body I can feel Nathaniel and talk to him as well, but that isn't enough to sustain me. I can't exist in a world where only one person has access to me. It's too possessive, too dependent, and I want more.

I walk directly to the warehouse. The streets are relatively quiet. Only the occasional car passes me as I walk through midtown. I don't realize until I'm across the street from it that the fire crews and investigators are gone and all that remains is a charred building.

It's easy to get in since I don't have a body to stop me. There's over an inch of water on the ground. It ripples around me as I walk, but I can't feel the moisture. I don't know what I hope to find by coming here, maybe a clue about Gage or Nathaniel, something that will help me figure out their next move. Wandering from room to room I find nothing.

I'm about to make my exit when bolt after bolt of electricity courses through me. Crying out in pain I crash to my knees and flop over onto my back. I try to flee, I try to jump to anywhere, into anyone, but I can't. The pain is too great. Twitching and writhing, I wish for death.

"That's enough!" a familiar, but distant voice yells.

"But this is fun," another voice whines. I recognize this voice as well.

Blinking and trying to focus, two shadows standing over me morph into solid images. Isadora and the girl who looks like Rae.

"Isadora, please," I beg.

"Bind her," Isadora instructs.

The Rae look-alike stomps down on my chest and then flips me over onto my stomach. She slips a thin metal strap around my wrists and ankles. They burn against my skin.

"Electricity," she tells me, as if she's reading my thoughts. "It makes you whole. This will keep you from breaching." She jabs a needle into my neck.

It's strange to be in this much pain and not be connected to a body. I lose consciousness.

When I wake I see that we're in another warehouse, one that's very similar to the one that burned to the ground. I attempt to find any means of escape, but even if I can find one, I won't get very far while tied up. I'm going to have to be patient and wait for my opportunity.

I'm pushed into a room. I skid across the floor.

The Rae look-alike unties my hands. "Feel free to try and jump." She laughs. "I enjoy watching you squirm."

She slams the door behind her.

It doesn't take me long to realize what kind of room I'm in. Gage took me to one just like it. It's jump proof. There's no means of escape.

I pace. I sit. I stand. The waiting is driving me crazy. The need to breach is eating at me like a craving. My hands are tingling and soon after, shaking. Gripping the sides of the cot, my legs jiggle up and down. I'll go mad if I stay here.

To calm myself, I sit, pull my knees to my chest, and close my eyes. The vibrating and pulsing worsens and I know I have to fight it. Deep breath in, deep breath out, and count to ten. Repeat.

Soon the rapid beating of my heart slows to a normal rhythm. The craving to breach, the need, it's still there, but

I have it under control and can suppress it. I just don't know how long I can keep it under control.

Suddenly the door bursts open. A woman is thrown inside. Before slamming the door again, the Rae look-alike says to me, "Happy homecoming."

Quickly, I rush to the side of the woman on the floor. She's unconscious, beaten, bruised, and barely breathing.

"Mom!" I cradle her head in my lap and brush the hair out of her face.

"Mercy," she croaks before her head lolls to the side and she's out again.

Chapter Thirty-Eight

Gage

There are too many abandoned buildings in Midtown. Nathaniel and I have been searching forever and each time we come up empty. We're losing time. Mercy could be dead by now. It's time to stop aimlessly searching and think.

"This is useless," Nathaniel yells, sharing in my frustration. "We're never going to find her like this."

"Give me a minute to think," I tell him.

"To think of what! We could spend the entire night searching and still come up with nothing. God knows what could be happening to Mercy right now."

"Don't you think I know that?"

"You're the damn Hunter! Why can't you think like one?"

Without the mark, I'm no longer a Hunter. But Nathaniel is right. It isn't as though The Assembled have stripped me of my memories. I still know how to fight and how to plan, how to think like a Hunter.

"I'm an idiot," I lament.

"Were you expecting an argument?"

"We've been searching in the wrong place. I don't know why I didn't think of this before! We've been assuming that The Assembled are hiding in a new warehouse and that's just what they want us to think. They're not at a new warehouse, they're at my warehouse."

Nathaniel and I set off running.

A block before the warehouse we pull up and do a check around. There are bound to be lookouts. Nathaniel signals to me that he spots one on the roof. He's heavily armed with weapons I recognize, because they're mine.

There are two more guards on the sidewalk in front of the building. I assume there are just as many behind. We're outnumbered and outmatched.

"This is a suicide mission," I say to Nathaniel.

"Most definitely, little brother."

Reaching into my jacket I take out my last two guns and hand one to him. There aren't many bullets, but we also have knives if we need them. Something tells me we will need them.

"On three. One. Two. Three."

We charge the entrance. Bullets fly in all directions. Nathaniel and I duck and weave. I feel heat in my arm as a bullet slices through my jacket. Nathaniel sees it too and he starts to make a move toward me. I shake him off. It's only a flesh wound. He lays down cover fire for me to advance to the doors. When I'm out of harm's way, I do the same for him. Once we reach the doors, we have to ignore the bullets from above and hope that the overhang will protect us. The guards are our main worry now. Nathaniel and I fight, trading and taking punches.

The boot of the man I'm battling hits me squarely in the jaw. I go down. My vision starts to cloud. Nathaniel rushes to my aide and defeats my attacker.

Extending his hand to me, Nathaniel pulls me to my feet. Together we dash into the building. Isadora and several guards are standing in a semi-circle just inside the door. Behind them are more men, all armed, all ready to kill.

"Hello boys," she says with a wry smile. "So glad you could join us."

We're surrounded.

"Where's Mercy?" Nathaniel asks.

Isadora's smile grows. Her features are disarming, her beauty unmatched by any human I've ever seen. She has the greenest eyes in creation, hair like silk, perfect skin, not a blemish or a wrinkle in sight. Beauty like this is never bestowed upon humans. Behind her beauty there's nothing but evil, and I only have to look deeper to see it.

"He asked you a question," I say to her. "Where's Mercy?"

"Paired up with a Breacher," Isadora says. "How quickly you've fallen."

A day ago, maybe even an hour ago, I would've felt guilty over my association with Nathaniel. But things have changed. I know that Nathaniel and Ariana were right all along. The Assembled are the problem. They're out of control and they need to be stopped.

Unflinching I say, "Isadora, tell me what you've done with Mercy."

"Don't worry, you'll have a ring side seat." Isadora motions to the guard. They respond quickly, grabbing and restraining us.

They force us down the hall and into a large room, one

that we previously used for extractions. I don't like the look of this. There are machines set up and trays of instruments: shiny and threatening scalpels, saws, tweezers, and the like. Nathaniel swallows hard and looks at me, the concern evident in his expression. There's something else about the way he looks at me, like he knows more than I do.

"What is all this?" I ask him quietly.

He averts his eyes for a moment. When he looks back at me he says, "We need to get her out of here." His tone is grave.

The guards shove us into chairs and bind us to them. Struggling against the binding is useless; they won't budge. Nathaniel has the same difficulty.

"We're just moments away from the big event," Isadora coos, her voice full of excitement. "You're going to want to stick around for this."

The guards stand at their posts, imposing pillars of terror who won't question Isadora's motives. They were created to follow orders, just like I was. Only they haven't been exposed to humans and so they have no humanity. There's no point in reasoning with them.

Whispering to Nathaniel I say, "Tell me what's going on. I know you know."

In all of my time chasing Nathaniel, I've never seen him look the way he does now. He's pained and frightened. He works his lips, pulling them in and out, grating them with his teeth because he doesn't want to tell me the truth. But it isn't that he relishes in keeping the information from me, like he would have before.

"Gage," Nathaniel's voice is empty, hopeless. "They're not going to kill Mercy. They're going to do something so much worse."

Chapter Thirty-Nine

Mercy

"Mom, please, please wake up."

She's no longer breathing. Will CPR work on someone like her? I don't know, but I have to give it my best shot. Titling her head back, I pinch her nose and blow breath into her mouth. Then I pump and pump her chest.

"You can't leave me," I beg. "You can't leave me!"

I can't let her die.

Regaining my composure, wiping the sweat from my brow, I tell myself to calm down and concentrate. Deep, yoga breaths. *Steady.*

I tap into something deep within me. For the first time, my power is willing to reveal itself. I see the scope of my abilities, understanding them now for the very first time.

I take a leap of faith and believe that I can do what I'm about to do.

With my left hand, I pierce my mother's chest, through

her flesh and past her rib cage until I hold her heart. Lightly, I grip the heart and squeeze over and over again, willing it to beat again.

The pull to breach her body entirely is strong. I know I don't have much time before I succumb to the need.

"Come on, beat!"

When her heart thumps against my hand, I rear back and slam myself against the wall. The humming, the urge, the need—it's all I can think about. The room is jump-proof, meaning I can't leave and breach somewhere else, but no one said anything about not being able to breach another body while inside the room.

Oh God. No!

It's like a magnetic force and fighting against it is beyond excruciating. Clawing at the walls, I'm unable to find a foothold.

"Mercy, don't." My mother's voice is weak. She's rolled onto her side and is trying to push herself up. "Fight it."

Scrambling, I push myself further away. "I can't."

"You can," she gasps. "I know you can."

Locking eyes with her, I tell myself that I don't want to breach, that I don't need to, that I'm safe. I keep inhaling and exhaling deeply, all the while staring at my mother, my mom who I haven't seen in six years.

The need to breach subsides slowly as the longing to be near my mom intensifies. We crawl toward each other and crash into an embrace.

"Baby girl," she breathes into my hair.

We cry together and cling to each other. She explores my face, runs her hands along my arms. Like I am with Nathaniel, I am whole around my mother even without a body.

"You saved me." She kisses my cheek. "My girl, my sweet

baby girl."

"What are they going to do to us?"

"Don't worry about that," she says. "I won't let anything happen to you."

I nod, believing her.

"You have more power than they do, Mercy. That's why I left. You have to know that. I didn't want them to find you, to use you like they used me. What do you know about The Assembled?"

"Only what Nathaniel and Gage have told me. That The Assembled is some sort of controlling body. Nathaniel told me about Ellie."

"They punished us, Mercy, for wanting to be human, for wanting to find love. They made us their slaves. I'm ashamed of what I did for them." She bows her head as she speaks. "I'm sorry."

"You didn't have a choice," I say to her.

She looks up and holds my face. "But you do."

"What do you mean?"

"There isn't time to explain it all. They'll be coming soon. You'll know what to do when the time comes."

She has such faith in me. It'll kill me to disappoint her.

The door opens and Isadora enters. "You lived," she says to my mother. "Good for you."

"If I hadn't ... " I start to say, but my mother grabs my arm, silencing me.

Isadora tilts her head and glares at me. "If you hadn't what?"

"Nothing," my mother answers for me. "She did nothing but hold me and whisper to me to come back."

"How sweet." Isadora's tone is mocking.

My mother doesn't want Isadora to know what I've done.

The Assembled must not know very much about me, or what I can do.

I was able to leave Lyla's body without killing her, which no one expected. I even breached a dead girl and brought her back to life.

What I did for my mother is so much more than breaching. If I was able to reach into her chest and start her heart, does that mean I can reach into a chest and stop a heart?

"On your feet," Isadora barks.

My mother is still weak and needs my assistance. I feel the burden of her weight as we follow Isadora. It's difficult to keep focused. Thinking of myself as solid helps a little, but with my mother pressing down on me I can feel myself blending into her. Luckily, we don't have far to go.

Isadora directs us into as room. As soon as I step in, two men take hold of me while a third sticks a syringe in my arm. I can't put up a fight as they strap me to the table. My heavy eyelids close. I struggle to keep them open.

Out of the corner of my eye I see Nathaniel and Gage tied to chairs across the room. They're both yelling, but I can't make out what they're saying. A fog surrounds my thoughts, preventing me from grasping anything.

A light goes on overhead. It burns my eyes. Squeezing them shut, I begin to wriggle on the table. The sounds hit my ears all at once: Gage yelling for me and screaming threats at the guards who stand by, my mother hurling insults at Isadora. Nathaniel stares at me, saying nothing. I think I see a tear streaming down his face.

Another needle plunges into my forearm. Again there's nothing but fog until Isadora leans over the table and says to me, "This is going to hurt."

Chapter Forty

Gage

"What are they giving her?" I ask Nathaniel for the third time, but he isn't responding. He's gone into shock. Tears careen down his face as he watches the horror unfold before us.

Mercy is drugged and not responding to our cries. With Nathaniel fading to my right and Ariana sobbing to my left, I know I have to act. I'm the soldier, the Hunter. I'm the one who has to put a stop to this. But fighting against the restraints is no use. Then I think maybe if I struggle enough I'll at least cause a distraction and buy us some time.

My plan is thwarted quickly as a guard backhands me across the face and tells me to be still. I am about to issue a threat to him when Rae enters the room. Rae. One look at her and all words are lost to me.

Rae, with her long, wavy blond hair and piercing blue eyes; she's standing right in front of me as if I had not seen her dead on the floor a few hours ago.

"Hello, Gage." She greets me before walking toward Mercy.

"You're dead."

She whips around and says, "You're partly right. Watch and learn."

Rae fiddles with a few instruments, making sure everything is to her liking. The anticipation of not knowing, but suspecting, what she's about to do, and knowing that there isn't anything I can do to stop her is killing me.

Selecting a scalpel, Rae moves to Mercy's left blocking our view. She raises her right arm and presses the blade into Mercy's ribs.

The scream that follows is deafening.

Mercy's body flops against the table like a fish on dry land. Guards move to hold her down.

Nathaniel is not looking at Mercy. His head is hanging down, a steady stream of tears drip from his chin to the floor. Ariana is struggling with all her might. Extra guards are brought in to hold her back as well.

Rae continues to work and Mercy screams again and then she goes limp. I can't see what Rae has in her hand, but I have an idea. She swaddles the item in muslin cloth and hands it off to an assistant. Then she stitches Mercy back together. I expect Mercy to react to the needle, but she doesn't even flinch.

"You can't do this!" Ariana shouts. "She hasn't done anything wrong!"

"It's done," Isadora answers flatly.

"What? What's done?" I ask Ariana.

She looks at me with sad eyes, with pity. "They've taken her rib."

"No!"

"Do you protest our little ritual, Gage?" Isadora feigns innocence. "Without it, you wouldn't exist."

This is what they did to Nathaniel? It's at that moment that I understand his pain. I understand why he hated me, why he hated them. They ripped part of his body away and from that they created me—the one ordered to hunt him down and kill him.

I no longer care what motive The Assembled may have had. This is wrong.

The white bundle containing the rib is removed from the room. I don't need Nathaniel or Ariana to tell me what happens next. I already know.

The rib will be cultivated and nurtured like a plant, given nutrients and special elixirs until it expands into an entire cage of ribs, beneath which a heart will grow. From there, blood from the donor would be injected into the heart and, with the help of machines, the heart will begin to pump. The rest of the body grows much like that of a baby. An incubator simulates that of a womb, but the growth rate is sped up, again with the help of elixirs, until a full-grown man or woman develops.

The DNA, although taken from the donor, is altered to create a super species that is faster, stronger and more adaptable. The entire process doesn't take long. Rae, Jinx, Zee, we'd all been born this way, and we never gave it much thought.

My whole life I thought I served a greater purpose, a greater cause. I'd never questioned that I was created from Nathaniel. It made sense to me that we should be created this way. What better way to stop someone than to create its copy, yet more powerful?

To know the truth now is maddening. To know that I'll

never be able to express my remorse, my sorrow to Nathaniel is more than I could handle.

It's time to act, to set things right. No longer will I sit by and let this happen.

"Isadora!" I shout. "You won't get away with this! I won't let you!"

She laughs like I've just said something exceptionally funny. "You sound just like him, you know." Isadora motions toward Nathaniel. "You were a test case, which clearly failed. I won't get it wrong this time."

"You're sick! Why are you doing this, torturing her like this when you could kill her and end it all now?"

"Where's the fun in that, love?" Isadora struts over to Mercy's lifeless body and runs her fingers along Mercy's leg. "Besides, I don't want Mercy dead. She's much more useful to us alive."

"She won't do what you ask!" Ariana yells.

"Why not? You did."

"Isadora, sister, listen to me," Ariana pleads. "Leave the humans. They don't need your interference. The wars, the murders, the bloodshed, to what end?"

"The humans don't want peace," Isadora answers. "They want war; they crave conflict. Lust, greed, mayhem; it's what makes them tick. It's what makes them human."

"This is all a game to you," I spit.

"And you are all my players," she says without even the faintest hit of guilt. "I'll give Mercy exactly what she wants, her body, her life as a human. And in return, she'll give me what I want—servitude. She'll breach for me and do my bidding and when her life runs out, I'll let her cross over."

Nathaniel's head snaps up and he roars, "Liar!"

Isadora marches over to Nathaniel and seizes him by the throat. With her face an inch from his she seethes. "You are the liar, Nathaniel Black. I gave you everything! And you betrayed me."

Confused, I look to Ariana hoping she might clue me in, but she offers nothing.

"My love was not yours to command, Is," Nathaniel says in a voice barely above a whisper.

Isadora's beautiful face contorts into an ugly grimace. "You chose that pathetic human when you could have ruled at my right hand. You will suffer for your choice from now until the end of time."

Casually, Isadora saunters over to Ariana and says, "Know this, sister. I might have let Mercy alone, might have done you that courtesy, but I couldn't sit by and let Nathaniel have her. He doesn't deserve leniency."

This is all about revenge? That's what Isadora really wants? It all makes sense now. Nathaniel was once Isadora's love. It wasn't just that Nathaniel fell in love with Ellie, that he broke the rules; it was that he spurned Isadora in the process.

Everything Nathaniel told me was the truth. The Assembled are not who I think they are. The reason I was created, to hunt and kill Nathaniel; there was no justice in it. My purpose was not for the greater good. My entire life was merely for the purpose of being a pawn in Isadora's sick game.

"Isadora!" I shout. "Let Mercy go! Now!"

"Absolutely anything for you, Gage." Isadora unhooks the restraints binding Mercy and with her entourage, including Rae, she leaves the room.

Chapter Forty-One

Mercy's body isn't moving. Nathaniel, Ariana, and I can do nothing but helplessly watch. The room is eerily silent as none of us even bother to breathe. All we can do is wait for a sign of life. And so we wait.

And wait.

"Her finger twitched," Nathaniel says suddenly.

"You're imagining it," I tell him. "I didn't see anything."

"Look again." Nathaniel motions toward Mercy.

Sure enough, Mercy's pinky moves ever so slightly. It's encouraging to know the procedure hasn't killed her. She's still for a long time. As I start to think we imagined seeing her finger twitch, she flexes her whole hand and opens her eyes.

"Mercy, can you hear me?" Nathaniel calls to her.

The three of us continue to struggle against the restraints, but clearly, we aren't having any luck. I've seen the video of both Nathaniel and Ariana bursting forth from the custody of

The Assembled and it's clear that improvements have been made since then.

Mercy moans and rolls onto her ride side, facing away from us. Slowly, with great effort, she sits up. She lets out a cry of pain and clutches her side.

"Mercy?" Ariana speaks softly, in a motherly tone.

Mercy tries to move, to get down off the table, but it's clear that every move she makes is agony. I want so desperately to help her. I don't need to ask Ariana or Nathaniel, I can tell by the way they lurch forward every time Mercy makes even the slightest movement that they want to help her as well.

Eventually, Mercy slides off the table. She holds her side the entire time. With short steps, she shuffles toward us.

"Mom?"

"Oh honey, it's me. I'm here. I'm so sorry." More tears spring from Ariana's eyes.

Confused, pained, Mercy looks to the three of us and asks, "What happened?"

There's a pause as none of us wants to be the one to explain.

Nathaniel breaks the silence. "Can you help me out of these?"

Mercy nods, but it's unclear whether she'll have the strength. If she's in great pain, and I assume she is, she doesn't let out another sound as she tirelessly works to free Nathaniel.

He bounds out of the chair like a puppy and scoops Mercy into his arms. She winces then melts into him while still holding her side. He closes his eyes and kisses the top of her head. A pang of jealousy surges in my chest, but I have to ignore it. Now is not the time.

Nathaniel carries Mercy to a nearby chair and gingerly lowers her into it. He kisses her again and whispers something

I can't quite hear before he returns to Ariana and me.

Deftly, quickly, Nathaniel undoes our restraints and the three of us rush back over to Mercy. Her eyes are closed and her head is lolled to the side.

Ariana kneels before Mercy and cups Mercy's face in her hands. "Sweet girl, can you hear me?"

Faintly, Mercy nods and mumbles, "Yes." She opens her eyes and holds her mother's gaze. "Mom," she says faintly.

Ariana cries against Mercy's thigh. "I'm sorry. I'm sorry."

The doors burst open interrupting their moment. Nathaniel and I assume a protective stance around them, but we're outnumbered and unarmed. There's nothing we can do to fight against the army that Isadora's fielded.

"Step aside," one of the more heavily armed guards barks.

Nathaniel and I exchange a look and then grudgingly moved apart.

"Get up," the guard orders. It's unclear who he's talking to, Ariana or Mercy. When Ariana stands and huddles near Nathaniel and me, the guard says again, "Get up."

Slowly, Mercy lifts her head. Her brown eyes are dull, her hair a mess. She looks like she's been through hell. She has. Clutching her side, Mercy rises from the chair and faces the guard. There's no fear in her expression; it's blank, cold.

Stepping out from behind the guards, Isadora faces Mercy head on. Mercy doesn't even flinch.

"You look terrible, my dear," Isadora says, feigning concern. "Why don't you come with me and I'll help you get cleaned up."

"No!" Ariana shouts.

Isadora tilts toward Mercy and says, "It wasn't really a question."

"What happens to them?" Mercy motions to where the three of us are standing. Her voice is gravelly and distant.

"That's not really your concern," Isadora informs her.

I start to force my way to her, but Mercy holds up her right hand.

"Gage, I know what I'm doing." She focuses her attention back to Isadora. "I'll make you a deal."

Isadora's left eyebrow arches and her lips curl into a curious smile. "I'm listening."

Mercy takes a deep breath and winces in pain. "Whatever it is you want from me, you can have it." Isadora's smile widens. "But you have to let them go." Isadora's smug smile disappears.

Mercy stands up straighter. It has to be agony to do so, but she isn't showing the strain on her face.

"You have to let them go and let them live. They'll live, they'll die, they'll cross over. That part of the deal is non-negotiable. They've suffered enough and they don't owe you anymore." Mercy's tone is forceful.

"No!" It's a collective shout, one that comes from me, Nathaniel, and Ariana.

Mercy ignores us. "Do we have a deal?"

"You can't trust her," Ariana warns.

"I don't," Mercy says. "So let me add this," Mercy continues. "If you break our deal, if any harm comes to them or anyone else that I love, I'll kill you. You and I both know that I can do it."

Isadora's eyes light up. It's unclear whether she's angry, fascinated, delighted, or a combination of all three. "You and I are going to have such fun together."

"Do we have a deal?" Mercy asks.

"Deal," Isadora quickly says.

Mercy walks slowly to the three of us. Neither the guards, nor Isadora protest. With her free arm she holds Ariana by the shoulder. Tears fill her eyes. "I love you. Say good-bye to Dad for me."

Ariana holds Mercy close, as close as Mercy allows, but Mercy quickly pulls back. She moves to stand before Nathaniel. His eyes are pleading and soft, full of love. She kisses him lightly on the lips and lingers there for a moment. I lower my gaze to the ground until I hope the kiss is over. When I look up again, Mercy is wiping his cheek and then she moves toward me.

My heart thumps heavily in my chest and my ears begin to ring. This heartache is like nothing I've ever felt before. Like a slow moving virus, the need to hold Mercy in my arms fills every inch of me.

"Gage," Mercy says softly. "I forgive you. I won't ever hold any of this against you. I need you to know that."

A lump rises in my throat. I don't know what to say.

"Look out for Lyla and Jay for me. Keep them safe."

"I will," I promise her.

Mercy kisses my cheek. Her wet eyelashes brush against my skin and I know right then that I love her, that my love for her will last forever and that even if it takes me forever, I'll find a way to get her back.

Mercy backs away from us and is about to join the guards when Nathaniel bursts forward and grabs her. The guards react and lunge forward, but stop on Mercy's command.

"I love you," Nathaniel says to Mercy. "I love you. Don't do this. We'll figure something out, please. Please!"

"I love you," Mercy replies. "I love all of you." She looks

to both Ariana and me. "Don't do anything stupid."

Mercy wriggles out of Nathaniel's grasp. Her hand is the last thing he clings to and then he finally lets go.

The guards sidestep and let Mercy pass. They fill in behind her so that we can no longer see her. Isadora gives us one last knowing look before she, too, leaves the room. The door bangs closed and the three of us are again alone and even more helpless than before.

Chapter Forty-Two

Mercy

With every step I take down the hall behind Isadora I steel myself a little more. I'm doing the right thing, the selfless thing, but that doesn't mean I'm not scared. But saving my mother, Gage, and Nathaniel—that's what keeps me moving forward. They've all done so much to protect me; they've risked their lives for me. It's time to repay them.

Isadora continues to lead the way down the long hall. Everything about this place is sterile and cold. From behind, Isadora very much resembles my mother. They are the same height, the same build, the same flowing hair, though Isadora's is streaked with deep black against the brown, whereas my mother's is auburn. Isadora has the appearance of a lovely woman, which gives a whole new meaning to the cliché— looks can be deceiving.

Isadora leaves me in a room that contains one small table and a rusty chair. She doesn't have to tell me what kind of room it is; I already know I won't be able to breach out of it.

When Isadora returns a few minutes later, she holds in her hand a syringe with a long needle.

"Give me your arm," she instructs.

Hesitating for only a second, I decide not to let her see me sweat. I extend my arm in her direction and don't flinch as she approaches. She grips my arm firmly and shoves the needle into my veins.

Isadora pushes the plunger and my body is on fire, burning and burning and just when I'm about to scream, she retracts the needle.

"It'll take a few minutes," she tells me.

"What will?"

She doesn't answer me.

"You can't win this, Isadora. You should know that by now."

"I've been one step ahead of you the whole time. You're sitting in that chair. I've already won."

I'm losing consciousness. With a heavy breath I force out a whisper. "Screw you."

And then she's gone.

Alone, I sink into the chair and put my head in my hands. Within seconds, I begin to feel strange, light headed and weightless. Struggling to keep my eyes open, I try to focus, to pull myself together, but it's useless. The urge to sleep is beyond my control.

When I open my eyes again, I'm home. My mom and dad are laughing in the other room and I go to join them.

"Well, there you are, sleepyhead." My mom's voice is syrupy sweet. "Late night?"

Thinking back, I can't remember what I did the night before. "I guess."

My father sips his coffee and thumbs through the newspaper. "Eight dead at the shopping mall on Arden. Such a tragedy."

"Senseless killings," my mother adds.

"Is there juice?" I ask, trying to change the subject.

"We have to talk about this, Mercy." My father closes the newspaper.

"Talk about what?"

"You can't go on like this, not if you want to live here," he tells me.

"I don't understand what you're saying."

My mother walks over to my father and puts her hand on his shoulder. "We thought we'd be able to handle this, you working for Isadora, but we can't do it anymore. You have to go."

Shocked, I try to defend myself. "But I did this for you, to save you."

"And while we appreciate that, honey," my dad pauses to take a sip of his coffee, "we don't think it's necessary that you live here. We wouldn't want the police tracing this back to us. Your mother and I have careers to think of, lives to lead."

"But I'm your daughter!" I yell. "You can't just kick me out onto the streets."

"Mercy, there's no need to shout," my mother scolds. "We understand the pressure you're under, we really do." My mother and father exchange a look. "But you made your choice and now you must deal with it."

I'm horrified by their words and lack of compassion. I can't believe what they're saying to me. They're my parents, the people who gave me life and they're casting me out like garbage. All the sacrifices I've made, all the deeds I've done for Isadora are to protect them, to ensure that they and everyone else that I love can lead a normal life. Was it all for nothing?

"This wasn't my choice," I say. "I had to do this! Isadora would've killed us all. You have to know that."

"Mercy, you could've been Isadora's downfall, but you didn't even try," Mother says.

I wait for them to laugh, to tell me that this is all a practical joke, but they just stare at me. My parents, the two people I love most in the world are discarding me without so much as a single tear. There's nothing left to say to them so I start to leave.

"Oh, Mercy, honey," my mother calls after me. "Don't forget your body."

"My what?"

"Your body, honey." Rising from his chair, my father walks over to a closet that hadn't been there moments before and from it withdraws my body, like he's taking a coat off the hanger.

The skin is grayish, zombie-like, with sores and scabs scattered about the arms and legs. The head is limp, the hair unwashed, greasy and tangled, in desperate need of a deep conditioning.

"That's my body?" I ask in disbelief.

"It's more like a skin suit at this point. Such decay," my mother tsks. "Not really worth the deal you made, is it, dear?"

This is the body Isadora gave me? I gave up everything for this? No way!

"No! No! No! No!"

Someone jostles my shoulder, but I continue to shout, "No!"

I shake again and this time I hear, "Mercy? Can you hear me?"

Though I want to wake up, to answer whomever it is that

calling me, I can't seem to climb out from under the haze. Like swimming through a swamp, the bottom pulls me under as I struggle for the surface. I'm weighted down with something, heavy clothing or maybe I'm wrapped in blankets.

My eyelids flutter. My eyes are sensitive and burn at the edges as if they haven't been used in a very long time. The pounding in my head is enough to make me drift back to sleep, but someone keeps calling to me and I know I have to stay awake.

My throat is impossibly dry and scratchy. I can't answer right away, but eventually I cough out, "Water."

Someone slides a straw between my lips. Water pools in my mouth, clean and yet also painful as it wets the back of my throat. It's like swallowing needles.

"Let's sit her up," someone says. It sounds like Nathaniel, but I can't be sure.

Several hands adjust themselves around me and hoist me into a sitting position. Unable to maintain being upright on my own, I lean into whomever is closest to me.

Languidly, my eyelids open and close until they remain open and I'm able to see the room around me. I nestle against Nathaniel with Gage and my mother standing across from me.

"Mom?"

She rushes forward. "I'm right here, baby."

Speaking takes much more effort than I anticipate and leaves my breath shallow and uneven. "What happened?"

Nathaniel holds me tightly against his chest. "We'll explain everything," he tells me. "You need to rest."

I try to protest, but I can barely move. Every part of me is so heavy. A prickling sensation begins at my toes and moves up my legs and into my stomach, across my chest and down my arms. I flex my hands and the joints crack as I stretch. Nathaniel eases his hold on me to give me space to move around.

"I feel so strange."

"Mercy, please, rest," Nathaniel urges me.

But I don't want to rest. I want to move around, to unclench. "Help me," I tell him as I struggle to get to my feet.

My mother and Gage both moved forward looking as if they're worried that I might collapse at any minute.

With my feet on the ground, I feel firmly rooted, connected. I know exactly what has happened to me.

I am back in my body. I'm in my bedroom. I'm home.

Chapter Forty-Three

Gage

A twinge of jealously bites me as Nathaniel wraps his arms around Mercy's waist. He holds her steady as she gingerly steps forward. Mercy's muscles are limp and tired from inactivity, though we're lucky that atrophy didn't fully kick in while she and her body were separated.

There are so many things I want to say to her, want to ask her, but I bite my tongue for the time being. Not wanting to overwhelm her or scare her are my two top priorities. Mercy and I will discuss everything once I know that she's adjusted to being back in her body.

This is what we all wanted, to return Mercy to her body. Unfortunately, we weren't expecting to pay this kind of price. When all is said and done, there's still much to worry about, namely the deal Mercy struck with Isadora. But there will be time for that worry later.

"How do you feel?" Ariana asks Mercy.

"Heavy." Mercy shuffles farther with Nathaniel's assistance. Watching him guide her I am, again, struck with a pang of envy.

"She let you go?" Mercy asks.

"That's the deal you made," I remind her.

Mercy's expression changes. Wrinkles crease her forehead as she pulls in her bottom lip.

"You need to rest," I tell her.

Mercy shakes her head, a look of defiance spreads across her face. "I'm strong enough." Her legs wobble, betraying her.

Ariana and I both lunge forward, but Nathaniel helps her before we can reach her. Mercy leans into him for only a second before she again takes a firmer stance.

Straightening her spine and cracking her neck, Mercy stands to her full height. Though she looks a bit war torn, she's still quite beautiful. Her hair is full and soft with brown waves that hang about her shoulders. Her cheeks are rosy again, regaining their natural color. Her pink lips and brown eyes invite me in. For a moment I am completely lost in thoughts of her, of her and me together, hand in hand.

Stop!

"We still don't know yet what Isadora's plan for Mercy is. It wouldn't be smart to act before gathering information." It's easier for me to act the part of the Hunter, the soldier.

"I know what her plan is," Mercy says. "And I know how to stop her."

"Did she tell you something?" Nathaniel asks. "Because you can't believe anything she says. It's all lies."

"She didn't tell me anything," Mercy tells us. "I just know."

Ariana wedges herself between Mercy and Nathaniel and ushers Mercy down the hall and into the living room. Nathaniel and I follow.

"I'm going to make us some tea," Ariana says once she's lowered Mercy onto the couch and covers her with a blanket.

"Mom, I'm not sick."

"You're not exactly well, either. Let me take care of you. It's been so long." Ariana's voice falters. She bends forward and kisses Mercy on the forehead.

When Ariana is out of the room, Mercy wriggles out from beneath the blanket. She's still struggling to breathe, as if she's forgotten that being in a body necessitates oxygen. She labors for a few more seconds and says, "We're going to destroy The Assembled."

Neither Nathaniel nor I move. We're both waiting for the punch line. But it doesn't come. Mercy is serious, and seriously delusional.

"That's impossible," I say. "You can't destroy The Assembled."

"Gage is right, Mercy. Taking on Isadora is one thing, but The Assembled? It can't be done."

Mercy smiles weakly. "I thought the same thing. I thought that everything was hopeless, but then I had this strange dream."

"You had a dream?" I ask her.

"Isadora injected me with something and I don't remember what happened after that, how she put me back into my body, anything. I was in a room and then I woke up here."

Nathaniel and I say nothing. We wait for her to breathe, for her to continue.

"In the dream, Isadora betrayed me. I went to work for her even though she lied to me and my parents tried to kick me out of the house."

So far, her dream doesn't tell me anything about how she plans to take on The Assembled. I'm trying to be patient and let her finish.

"My dream parents kept talking about my choice, how I chose to work for Isadora when I could've chosen differently. And they're right. I can choose differently. I don't have to keep my deal with Isadora."

"I'm not sure I'm following you," I say to Mercy. Judging by the look on Nathaniel's face, he isn't following her either.

"I'm the one, the one to end it all."

Mercy lets the words hang there out in the open for Nathaniel and me to soak in, for us to try and interpret the underlying meaning.

"Mercy, you've been through a lot, but let's be reasonable," Nathaniel tries, but Mercy waves him off.

"Think about it," she says. "Why would Isadora come after me so vigilantly? Do you really believe it was all about revenge? That she's just a scorned lover?"

Mercy has a point. Isadora is going to a lot of trouble if her only goal is to get back at Nathaniel.

"This isn't about Nathaniel, and it isn't some sick game she's playing. She doesn't want me to find out the truth about myself, about what I can really do. But I found out anyway and I know what I have to do now."

Before I can stop myself, I ask, "What do you have to do?"

Mercy looks directly at me and without faltering says, "I'm going to breach The Assembled. And then I'm going to kill each one of them."

She's crazy. Something is seriously wrong with her. Breach The Assembled? It's insane! It can't be done. The Assembled cannot be breached because they are not human, they are not susceptible to such things.

Stealing a quick glance at Nathaniel, I know he's thinking the same thing, that it's impossible. Breaching The Assembled is not the way to end Isadora's reign of terror. There has to be some other way to take her down.

"Mercy," I say, "you can't breach an immortal. It can't be done." I look to Nathaniel for support. "Right?"

"Gage is right. If breaching an immortal were possible, it would've been done already, or at the very least, someone would've tried." Nathaniel clears his throat and adds, "I would've tried."

"Do you trust me?" Mercy poses the question to the room.

"It's not a matter of trust, Mercy," I'm trying my best to sound comforting. "It's just that it can't be done."

"You don't know that," she replies.

"We do know. Believe me, it's not possible." Nathaniel sits next to Mercy on the couch. He takes her hand and kisses her knuckles and I cannot help but look away. "We'll find a way to fight Isadora, I promise."

Mercy withdraws her hand and her denial of Nathaniel's affection pleases me more than I am willing to let myself admit.

Pushing off the couch, Mercy stands and Nathaniel immediately mirrors her movements. Though I hate it, it's a good thing he does because Mercy is still unable to stand on her own. With his hand on her elbow, Nathaniel holds her steady.

"Mercy, you need to take it easy," he says to her. She gives him a look. "Please," he adds.

"Fine." Mercy relents and sits back down on the couch.

Ariana returns with the tea and she immediately senses the

tension in the room. "What's going on?"

"Nothing," Mercy quickly answers.

Mercy takes the mug from Ariana and blows on it until it's cool enough for her to take a sip. We sit together, saying nothing, while Mercy sips her tea. Neither Nathaniel nor I clue Ariana into our conversation. I'm certain if we had, she'd have told Mercy the exact same thing Nathaniel and I had, that breaching an immortal is impossible.

As we sip the tea, the front door opens and Mercy's father walks in. He stares with disbelief at the sight of us all. For a moment I think he might faint.

"Eric." Ariana slowly moves to him. Her level of control impresses me. She puts her hand on his face and his eyes close at her touch.

He covers her hand with his and then they are embracing. Mercy's eyes well until the tears spill over.

When they finally pull apart Eric focuses his attention on Mercy. He rushes to her and folds her into his arms. More tears run down her cheeks as she holds him tight.

I motion to the door and Nathaniel and I duck outside. We've intruded enough on their private moment. It's time to give them some peace.

Once we're outside, we begin to walk. We pass a few houses before I ask the inevitable question, the one I know I'm not going to like the answer to.

"Do you think she can do it? Breach The Assembled?"

Nathaniel keeps walking, eyes forward. "Yes."

"You said yourself it's not possible," I remind him.

"If it is possible, Mercy is the one to do it. Think about it, Gage, everything we thought we knew about Breachers has been blown to shit since we met Mercy. She can do things we thought were impossible. Why shouldn't she be able to do this?"

I stop walking and turn to face him. "Are you going to tell her?"

"I don't know."

The only thing I know for certain is that we have to stop Isadora. Nathaniel and I will return to Mercy's house eventually. We'll formulate a plan and we'll carry that plan to fruition. Maybe we'll live, maybe we'll die; there's no way of knowing for sure. What I do know is that wherever Mercy goes, I will follow.

Chapter Forty-Four

Mercy

My family is whole again. The embraces last for a long time. When Lyla, Jay, and Kate arrive we start up again. Hugs, kisses, lots of tears, it's everything I could want and more. Though I know this moment of bliss is fleeting, I bask in it, reveling in the realization that I've gotten everything I've ever wanted.

Isadora will come for me eventually. It's the bargain I struck with her—I do her bidding and she lets my family alone. Will I be able to stomach the jobs I'm tasked with? Probably not, but if it means I get to keep my family, I'm willing to try.

There is also option B. Though both Gage and Nathaniel are convinced that breaching The Assembled is impossible, I know in my heart that they are wrong. I also know in my heart that I am not strong enough to do it yet. Working for Isadora will give me access to The Assembled and it'll give me the information I need. I may not be able to breach The Assembled now, but someday I will. And when I do I know that I'll have Gage and Nathaniel by my side.

Someday, when the time is right, I will tell them how I saved my mother, how I reached into her chest and started her heart. It will be the definitive proof they need. Once they understand my abilities, they'll know that I'm capable of anything, including breaching an Assembled.

What I'm still unsure of is whether or not, once I breach them, they'll be able to fight me off from the inside. Breaching Kate and Lyla's bodies taught me that I am able to connect with the soul that belongs in the body. I saw Lyla's memories. I heard Kate's voice telling me how to drive a car. They were there with me. Will it be the same with an Assembled? And if it is, what will that be like? I seriously doubt they'll be as welcoming and forthcoming. It isn't the breaching part that gives me pause; it's everything that comes after.

Later that night my dad cooks dinner and my mom and I do the dishes. It's like nothing has ever changed and she and I aren't Breachers. We aren't beings that don't belong in this world; we're just ourselves and it's wonderful.

After dinner, my mom and dad retreat to their bedroom. Not wanting to be grossed out forever, I decide to go for a walk and give them time alone. It's on the sidewalk, not too far away from my house that I meet up with Nathaniel and Gage.

"You're smiling," Gage notes.

Laughter escapes me, real, honest laughter. "I can't seem to stop."

Nathaniel smiles at me. "It suits you," he says.

"I feel like a kid. My parents are back together and that makes everything better, safer somehow." I slip my hands into the pocket of my jeans. "I know that sounds stupid considering everything we've been through and everything we're facing, but … " I don't quite know how to finish my thought.

"That's not stupid," Gage says with deep affection in his tone.

Kicking at the sidewalk with the toe of my shoe, I muster up the courage to say what I need to say.

"Um." I clear my throat. "I want to say thank you to both of you, for everything. You saved my life, more than once. And you brought my mother back to me." My voice catches in my throat.

"You don't have to thank us," Nathaniel tells me. "We'd do anything for you."

"Anything," Gage adds.

An awkward silence follows. Not knowing what else to say, I blurt out, "I think we should celebrate."

They're both taken aback by my suggestion.

"Celebrate?" Gage questions me.

"Why not? We've been through hell and we survived."

"Shouldn't we talk about what we're going to do about Isadora?" Gage, ever the soldier, is ready to get down to business.

Nathaniel claps him on the back. "Tomorrow, brother. Tonight, we celebrate."

It's decided. We head to Wally's and meet up with Kate, Lyla, and Jay. The future still looms before us and there's plenty of danger ahead, but in this moment we're friends, hanging out and laughing the night away.

The End

ACKNOWLEDGEMENTS

There was a time when I'd given up on this book, when I'd decided to tuck it in a file and forget it even existed. Luckily, a wonderful mentor and friend prodded me along until the story finally morphed into something publishable. I am eternally grateful to Georgia McBride for the loving push forward into publishing. There are not enough ways to express my gratitude.

Thank you to everyone at Month9Books for your love and support. I couldn't have asked for my book to have a better home. I am honored to be part of the Month9 family.

To my family, my husband John, my daughters Izzy and Maddy, thank you for letting me ignore you so that I can write. Thank you for being there for me, for holding my hand, and for supplying me with fuzzy socks to go with my yoga pants. You really do get me.

Thanks Mom and Dad for buying all of my books. Sorry there's so much swearing in this one. Love you!

Of course I can't write this section without thanking my friends. Jennifer Toy, Jill Rice, I could not do this without you. Thank you for loving me and the voices in my head. Thank you for letting me ramble on about my characters and for keeping me from taking a baseball bat to my computer when things weren't going well. I am so lucky to call you both friend. I can still do that, right?

CAROLINE T. PATTI

Caroline T. Patti is the author of *The World Spins Madly On* and *Too Late To Apologize*. When she's not writing, she's a school librarian, mother of two, wife, avid reader and Green Bay Packer fan. You can chat with her on Twitter at https://twitter.com/carepatti or find her on Facebook at https://www.facebook.com/pages/Author-Caroline-T-Patti/33592507779.

OTHER MONTH9BOOKS TITLES YOU MIGHT LIKE

HUNTED
WHERE THE STAIRCASE ENDS
VESSEL

Find more awesome Teen books at Month9Books. com

Connect with Month9Books online:
Facebook: www.Facebook.com/Month9Books
Twitter: https://twitter.com/month9books
You Tube: www.youtube.com/user/Month9Books
Blog: www.month9booksblog.com
Request review copies via publicity@month9books.com

THE SINNERS SERIES

HUNTED

ABI KETNER & MISSY KALICICKI

STACY STOKES

WHERE
THE
STAIR
CASE
ENDS

A NOVEL